T0368085

PUBLISHED WORKS

"THE JUMP"
"RETURN TO THE CITY"
"LIFE CHOICES—ASSIGNMENT FROM GOD"
"LITTLE MESSENGER"
"THE CABINS"

THE CABINS

Jayda Lee Wilson

"Then the King will say to those on His right hand, 'Come, you blessed of My Father, inherit the kingdom prepared for you from the foundation of the world: for I was hungry and you gave Me food; I was thirsty and you gave Me drink; I was a stranger and you took Me in; I was naked and you clothed Me; I was sick and you visited Me; I was in prison and you came to Me. Then the righteous will answer Him, saying, 'Lord, when did we see You hungry and feed You, or thirsty and give you drink? When did we see You a stranger and take You in, or naked and clothe You? Or when did we see You sick, or in prison, and come to You?' And the King will answer and say to them, 'Assuredly, I say to you, inasmuch as you did it to one of the least of these My brethren, you did it to Me.'"

Matthew 25:34-40 (NKJV)

WESTBOW
P R E S S®
A DIVISION OF THOMAS NELSON
& ZONDERVAN

WestBow Press books may be ordered through booksellers or by contacting:

WestBow Press
A Division of Thomas Nelson & Zondervan
1663 Liberty Drive
Bloomington, IN 47403
www.westbowpress.com
844-714-3454

ISBN: 979-8-3850-3554-0 (sc)
ISBN: 979-8-3850-3555-7 (e)

Library of Congress Control Number: 2024920891

Print information available on the last page.

WestBow Press rev. date: 11/04/2024

CONTENTS

CONTENTS

NOTE FROM THE AUTHOR

What do a cabin, shots fired, a cell, and Jesus have in common? Turn the pages to see how prayer and evangelism can make a difference in a life under the worst conditions.

This was a different type of book for me to write since I had never written scenes with violence in them, so I wasn't sure how it was going to go. I faltered in the direction of the story, until it became apparent that the Holy Spirit was taking charge of the narrative, there was a plan, I just didn't know what was expected. It was impressive how He twists the story around and had Jesus show up on the scene. The events that take place are not as foreign a subject as one might think. Supernatural occurrences happen today, all around us, without us being aware. Keep an open mind, stay focused on the Scriptures, and enjoy the journey.

Music is submitted at the end of most of the chapters, when I was directed to enhance the story with song. I hope that you will take the time to listen and be inspired by the lyrics and the melody. One such song that touched me was "Nobody" by Casting Crowns. This song seems to fit the main character in this story so well, it brought me to tears when I heard it and thought of Zach, the young man in the story.

What I am blessed with, I will share with others. Donations from this book will go towards prison ministries. I haven't been called to that type of ministry, but I have a heart towards those that need to hear about Jesus, therefore I am happy to support other's efforts in spreading the Gospel of Jesus in these places. After reading this book you may also feel compelled to support such a ministry. May you be blessed by the message as well as the journey through this story.

A special thanks to my family and friends for their continued support of my work which I consider my ministry. I couldn't have made it this far without the help of my dear friend Lori and the continued patience and encouragement of my husband.

Jayda Lee Wilson

1

SHOTS FIRED

There is a destination spot in the North Carolina mountains, where many like to go to explore the outdoors and get back to nature. It's called The Cabins. Many are rentals and some are simply owned as individuals' mountain homes for their own getaways. They are tucked away in the mountains for privacy and a bit of wilderness style living, each cabin sits on approximately five acres or more. Allowing for privacy yet not seclusion.

The Johnsons are one of the families that have their own cabin, used strictly as their family retreat. They have spent many adventurous weekends in the mountains, and at least a week is spent at the cabin in the summer and in the fall. The cabin is owned by George Johnson, better known as Pop, the grandfather to Elsie, a spirited four-year-old. George had been entertaining Elsie outside, while Ellen and Chris packed their things after finishing up their week at the cabin. It had been a great family time, putting all other cares aside to spend quality time with each other. This had been a family tradition since Ellen was a little girl.

After the death of Mrs. Johnson a few years back, a lot of adjustments had to be made. It had been hard without her, especially for George, but it was easier to cope with the emotions when they were all together and could share memories of her. It was especially helpful to George to have others around, to help him overcome his loneliness. These trips to The Cabins gave him something to look forward to.

Pop and Elsie came through the back door, which entered the rear bedroom, where her parents were finishing gathering their things. Elsie was rushing to use the one and only bathroom in the cabin, located right off the main bedroom. It was a large bathroom with a big cast iron tub, which Elsie considered her personnel playground.

There was plenty of fun pretending that she was getting baptized in the big tub, with plenty of sloshing and waterfalls from the tub's edges. She had seen the dunking taking place at church and thought that it looked like great fun to explore the depths of the pool. However, she must have officially baptized herself in the big iron tub at least a hundred times. A great love for the Lord was evident, because she talked about Jesus all the time, to anyone who would listen to her.

Ellen, her mom had been good about taking their everyday life situations and talking with her about what the Bible says regarding those moments. Elsie claimed Jesus must have known about everything, but mostly all about her life, the way her mom was always pointing out the correlations.

A lot of kids have imaginary friends, Elsie has Jesus. She talks with Jesus and has Him over for tea on Fridays, explaining that Saturdays and Sundays are quite busy for Him. Ellen loves to hear Elsie's childhood banter, or conversations she has with Jesus, over tea. It warms their hearts that she has embraced Jesus as her friend.

A schoolteacher by trade was Ellen's profession before Elsie was born. She had quit teaching in the public schools to stay home with her baby and to aid in the care of her mother during her last days. It was time well spent, her mother got to see the baby as often as she liked and had spoken blessings over her every visit. Every moment was cherished with her mother, and she had promised her that she would home school Elsie, as long as she could. This had proven to be the right course for Elsie because she was a fast learner and Ellen could work her at her own pace and skill level.

Dancing her way to the bathroom, Elsie's mom helped her on the potty after stripping off her shorts. Ellen could tell she had enjoyed herself in the creek, maybe a little too much, as she turned and eyed Pop, the one that was supposed to keep her clean for the ride home. Pop looked the other way, avoiding the look that he had received, hoping that he didn't get in any trouble from his daughter. However, he just couldn't avoid getting a tongue lashing that he deserved.

"Thought you were to watch her, Pop, not allow her to get this dirty, and right before we leave. She's going to have to change clothes now. And I'm going to have to haul these dirty things home."

"I was watching her; she had a great time." He smirked back at her.

Smiling and turning to leave the bathroom to give the girls a little privacy, as he hid his little chuckle. Their playground was the creek and the grassy hillside just beyond the deck of the cabin. She loved to roll down the hill into Pops arms. He was sure the grass stains would come out of the clothes. Ellen was aware of the fun she had because she had the same play area when she was a child. But she was the one now, cleaning up the mess afterwards. Apparently, her mom had to contend with the same things. Pop had no idea of the trouble they went through to keep their clothes clean.

Ellen rolled her eyes at Elsie. "Considering you are half undressed; I might as well rinse you in the tub."

Squeals of joy erupted from Elsie, who thought that meant playtime in the big tub, her favorite thing to do. When suddenly shots were heard. Then additional rounds were reverberating from a distance. Pop and Chris looked at each other and had the same thought, that's gunshots, for sure.

They walked out onto the deck, just outside the bedroom, to see what was happening. Pop looked in one direction and Chris in the other, trying to determine the direction of the shots. Then another shot was fired. It caught both of their attention, swinging their heads to the north. Looking up the hill, they saw two men walking out of the cabin north of them with what looked like firearms. They both froze for a second, after witnessing those two men shooting someone that was fleeing to a golf cart.

"What on earth is going on?"

"Is that some domestic dispute, turned deadly?"

"Doesn't matter, we just witnessed a murder. We need to get help."

Their hearts stopped when they saw the two men change course, now coming in their direction.

"Did they see us?" Chris stated as he pushed his body back against the cabin.

"Why are they coming over here? Wouldn't they be fleeing the crime scene?"

Shocked by the event, terror shot through Pop wondering what they were going to do to protect them against armed men. Pop and Chris eased inside the door and locked it, then went into the bathroom giving the signal to be quiet. Ellen knew something was wrong, she had heard the shots, but was unaware that they were about to be the next to be intruded upon. Chris didn't think that a locked door would stop them from entering, nor could he remember if the front door was even locked. There was no vehicle to indicate occupancy at their cabin.

If they came in to search the cabin, they might see their bags packed and assume someone is present. If they were fortunate, at first glance they may not see the bags, located on the other side of the bed, where he had just slid them off and onto the floor, ready to roll out the door. Pop didn't have luggage; it was his cabin, which he kept equipped with what he needed for his stays so that he didn't have to carry things up the hill.

The car wasn't outside, because most of the cabins were required to park in a central parking lot below the cabins. Carts were always available to use to push your bags up to the cabins, or just hike down meandering paths. A few cabins had golfcart paths for handicap access, or for those who had cabins a bit further from the parking lot area.

When their footsteps were heard on the front deck which wrapped around the cabin, Chris motioned for Ellen to get into the tub with Elsie and keep their heads down. He directed Pop to crouch down behind the tub the best he could, and pull the hamper in front of him, the tub would possibly shield them from gunfire. While he hid in the large linen closet, located in the bathroom. It may have seemed like a flimsy plan, but it was all that he could muster in such a short time.

If shots were fired, he would count on the iron tub to protect his wife and child. Hoping that if he had to, he was in a position to surprise them by jumping out to protect his family. He threw the towel to Elsie to cover herself and took the towel rod as a makeshift weapon.

He was thankful now that the cabin was built with such deep closets in all the rooms, including the bathroom, he was not a small man, so it made for a tight fit. It had been a must by Mrs. Johnson during construction years ago. They didn't want a large cabin, but each room was to be spacious, including the closets. The cabin was a two-bedroom, one bath design. The deck wasn't constructed until Chris joined the family. They believed they would spend most of their time outside on the deck with the family growing, so he and Pop built a wraparound porch, that took a couple of summers to complete.

The two men entered the front door, knocking things over and searching for money or anything of value. Chris and his family remained very quiet; hearts were pounding with each footstep. Elsie was confused and wanted to get out of the big tub now, it was no longer fun. It was crowded in the tub, and she was being squeezed. Ellen didn't speak, she just shook her head indicating no, and gave Elsie a very serious look. Picking up on the fact that her mom was scared, she burrowed into her mom more and kept quiet.

A woman's voice was heard. Chris was trying to make out what was being said. There was nothing of value in their cabin, most of what was there only had emotional significance to them. It didn't sound as if they were going to dash through the house and move on. It sounded more like they were settling in. This could only mean trouble for the family.

Chris's concern heightened for his family, how was he going to protect them with only a rod in his hand? The verse that came to him was, "*You shall break them with a rod of iron; You shall dash them to pieces like a potter's vessel* (Psalm 2:9 NKJV)." God would have to provide the skill and strength needed to defend his family, at this moment. He had hoped these murderous people would find whatever they were looking for and move on, and his family could somehow escape this terror.

These men approaching the family cabin had stolen small valuables from the other cabins and apparently had shot anyone in sight, leaving a trail of bodies over the mountainside. This was information unknown to the family, but they had witnessed a man being shot, so they knew that these individuals were dangerous.

The next cabin in their line of sight appeared empty, having moved away from the other cabins with dead bodies lying around, they decided to stay the night in the less occupied cabin before moving on. It was clear that they showed no fear of being caught, they moved about nonchalantly, without a care.

Chris couldn't hear any discussion regarding them fleeing the mountainside, apparently, they were in no hurry to vacate the area. Why would they linger around such a heinous crime scene? Now trying to think, how many cabins had been rented or were occupied over the weekend?

How many cabins had these people entered? Did they know the victims that they shot or was it random?

How many people were caught up in this tragedy? Would they be next? Would the cleaning crews from the rental properties come across the bodies? When would they be coming to do their cleaning? How long would Elsie be able to remain quiet?

This was a time for silent prayers to be lifted. Psalm 32:7,8 (NASB) came to mind. *"You are my hiding place; You preserve me from trouble; You surround me with songs of deliverance. I will instruct you and teach you in the way which you should go; I will counsel you with My eye upon you."*

Ellen was silently crying, tears rolling down her face, gripped with fear, wishing that they had left a day earlier. Realizing the danger that they were in, it was like being a kid again, glad that her father was nearby, he had reached around the tub and was patting her shoulder for comfort. There was an aching for her mother's wisdom and was thankful for her mother encouraging her to memorize Scripture verses.

It never occurred to her that she would need to lift prayer under these circumstances. She realized now that she wouldn't always have a Bible close by to refer to, therefore it was important to have God's Word in your heart. Her mother had always told her that the Lord likes for us to repeat His Word to Him, there is power in His Word.

With a silent prayer she lifted the words she knew. *"Deliver me, O my God, out of the hand of the wicked, Out of the hand of the unrighteous and cruel man. For You are my hope, O Lord GOD; You are my trust from my youth. By You I have been upheld from birth; You are He who took me out of my mother's womb. My praise shall be continually of You* (Psalm 71:4-6 NKJV)."

It was not a matter of whether she would lay down her life for her family, it was a matter of how she was to protect them, at all costs. Was she to offer herself up as a prize to these two men as a distraction, while the others ran for cover in the woods? Eventually they would come into this bathroom and notice them. There was no way to discuss a plan with her husband without being heard. If she moved around in the tub, it could create noise. She knew that the tub was suggested for cover in case they started shooting, but now it seemed they were trapped in the tub.

It was felt that Chris was going through the same emotions that she was experiencing. She knew her husband to be a brave man, but how was he to fight off bullets? It may come to the wiles of a woman to bargain for the life of her family. The courage would have to be summoned to do what was necessary. The verse that came to mind was Joshua 1:9 (NIV) *"Be strong and courageous. Do not be afraid; do not be discouraged, for the LORD your God will be with you wherever you go."*

While still hunkered down in the closet Chris was trying to think of a strategy to save his family. The verse that kept rolling around in his head as some kind of encouragement was Jeremiah 15:20,21 (NKJV), *"And they will fight against you, But they shall not prevail against you; For I am with you to save you And deliver you, says the LORD. I will deliver you from the hand of the wicked, And I will redeem you from the grip of the terrible."*

They are certainly gripped in terror right now, and it was apparent that they would be fighting their way out of this. But he was believing that evil will not prevail, they have God on their side. Chris knew that words can be powerful, they hold the ability of life and death. If he was given the opportunity to talk with these men, he would have to measure his speech carefully. Remembering Proverbs 15:1 (NKJV), *"A soft answer turns away wrath, But a harsh word stirs up anger."*

Chris was thankful that he had God's Word in his heart and could rely on Him in times of trouble. He just never thought he would find himself in this kind of situation. Sharing God's Word with others was something that came natural to Chris. He was a skilled craftsman, much like Jesus, who sought out the opportunity to share the Gospel with those he encountered. Being in his line of work, he encountered people from various walks of life, from a fellow contractor to the CEO of a corporation. If given an opportunity he would share his faith with these men just as he has shared with others.

The two men in the other room were hooting and hollering about the loot they had collected for the day. The woman had been quiet, until the point where she raised her voice and told them to settle down. It was clear that she was in charge, when one of them called her mom, he realized they were family. Orders were being barked out about picking up the furniture they had turned over, so that they had a place to sit. One was ordered to find firewood for a fire, while the other one looked for something to eat in the kitchen.

Chris figured this was the time to whisper some directives to his family, while they were making noise through their movements creating the fire and rustling in the kitchen. He hoped that when he started to whisper, it didn't get Elsie stirred up to think that she could start talking. He opened the closet door and put his finger to his lips to signal that they needed to remain quiet.

Then he shared in a soft whisper, "Once he comes in with the firewood from the front, we need to make a move to the back door."

Further explaining that Pop needed to go first, he would bring up the rear. If anyone was able to break free and run, go for it, and don't look back, was the messaging. Directive was to go for help. It was hard to discuss the reasons for his plans, so he was hoping that they were reading his mind to some degree. There wasn't time to share alternative plans or suggestions.

Thinking that if Pop got free, he knew the woods well, and could make it to town, or to the nearest home for help. If they were to see him, then he was out front as a diversion so that the others could escape. It was all risky. Chris would have to fight off anyone coming after them from the rear, it was his job to be a human shield for them. There was no doubt that he would take a bullet for his family, and he would fight with whatever was available to him. Praying that God gave him the strength to fight off two men at once.

Ellen needed to provide cover for Elsie, however, and wherever she could find it, even if it came down to one of the other cabins littered with bodies. Hearts were racing, adrenaline rushing through their veins, getting them pumped for what they were about to face. Chris was very proud of his little girl. She had remained quiet and alert to what was going on.

When they were about to make their move, the bedroom door opened which threw their plans off. The mother had walked into the bedroom and was looking around. It was feared that she may have seen the luggage. Pushing the bathroom door open, as if she was expecting someone to jump out at her. A sign that she was aware now that someone could be in the cabin. Everyone remained still.

She walked into the bathroom with darting eyes, looking around the room as if surveilling it, noticing them in the tub, but didn't say anything. It was clear that she had the upper hand, with her two boys armed and dangerous, just outside the door. Upon noticing a little girl, she remained quiet, as a plan was culminating in her head.

It was time to react. Chris couldn't miss this opportunity to take her hostage or take her down. It bothered him to attack a woman, but she was the one in charge, it was a matter of protecting his family. He had to summon the courage and strength needed to act quickly. He swung the door open from the closet, startling her enough for him to grab and gag her before she let out a shout. That's when Ellen and Elsie jumped out of the tub, Pop darted out the back door first as instructed, Ellen grabbed Elsie and wrapped her in the towel, following after her father. The two men heard the activity in the back of the house and came running.

Chris threw the woman on the bed with a harsh push, while tripping one man up, causing him to fall to the floor and struggling with the other. The man that was tripped, got up and ran outside yelling for Ellen to stop, as he fired a shot in the direction of Pop. Ellen screamed watching her father fall. Her heart felt as if it had stopped beating. Shock set in; she was overwhelmed by the traumatic event.

The woman from inside, yelled instructions not to hurt the child. The man didn't bother to go after Pop, he just grabbed Ellen and Elsie, and drug them back inside as instructed like rag dolls. When Chris saw that they had not gotten away he gave up the fight, so that his girls wouldn't be harmed. This broke him, he thought that Ellen would have been able to break free and hide somewhere, even if it were under the cabin, but she was traumatized by the gunfire and watching her father fall to the ground. Seeing how confused she was, now had him worried about her state of mind.

The mother directed Zach, the young man holding onto Ellen and Elsie, to throw them on the bed. The other man, Jasper, was picking himself up off the floor and pulling out his weapon pointing it in Chris's direction with furry.

Ellen screamed, "No!"

Her mind couldn't take another catastrophe, she was struggling to make sense of the situation she was in now. One minute she was crying and the next she felt powerful enough to stand up against these thugs. Apparently experiencing an emotional rollercoaster.

"What have we here? A little family with a feisty woman." Jasper was eyeing Ellen in a lustful way when his mother told him to back off. There were other plans that needed to play out first.

The mother's attention was on Elsie, a little girl that she never had, yet longed for. An opportunity arose for her to take this little girl under her wing. It was not her intention to scare Elsie, she wanted to befriend her, she was a very deceptive and cunning woman. And what better way to befriend a scared child, than to show some compassion toward her parents, until the right time. Instructions were given to the boys to secure the parents and then her focus was returned to Elsie.

"Honey, you need to get some proper clothes on." She looked at Ellen and asked where her things were.

Ellen pointed in the direction of the luggage, barely able to think clearly. The mother walked over and opened the luggage and pulled out some clothes for Elsie as if she was going to dress her up like a doll. Ellen was still shaken from her father being shot. She couldn't believe they were just going to leave him laying out there.

It was more than she could comprehend. She had heard the other gun shots but had not witnessed any one being killed in cold blood. This was difficult for her; it was her father. The feeling of being lost and alone engulfed her. It had been an uneasy process journeying through grief over her mother's death and now she witnessed her father being killed before her eyes. This was all too devastating for her to come to grips with.

"Do you like these?" The woman asked Elsie in a sweet voice, holding up a little outfit.

Elsie just nodded in the affirmative, still dazed and in a little shock herself. Walking around the bed she proceeded to help Elsie get dressed. Assisting her like a grandmother would. Speaking sweetly to Elsie, trying to give her some comfort.

Upon asking her what her name was, she gave her own name. "I'm Louise, we are going to be good friends."

Further instructions were given to the boys for the benefit of Elsie. "Now boys, you need to be nicer to these people. We are guests in their house. Jasper, go get that fire started, this child is freezing."

The boys were thinking their mom had lost her mind. They did not understand their mothers' plans, but it was apparent that she was up to something.

Song "I'll Be Okay" by Lydia Laird

2

CONFUSION

There was confusion among all parties involved, except the mother. She knew exactly what she was doing and what she wanted. Ellen was too dazed with grief to understand what was taking place. Chris was watching what was going on but wasn't sure what to make of their situation. The boys looked as if this were something different for their mother, her actions were out of the ordinary. She never doted on anyone, at least not that they ever noticed. She ruled with an iron fist, to control them and keep them close to her.

Chris continued to observe their every move carefully not knowing when they might turn on him, having already shot Pop why would they hesitate to shoot him. It was obvious they don't mind killing those who stepped in their way. He wanted to be alert to at least try to defend himself and Ellen.

The older son had shown an interest in Ellen, which raised concern, and the mother had attached herself to his daughter. There were obvious intentions of kidnapping her. As much as the thought caused him to ache, he found peace that they wouldn't kill her. He was assuming, at this point, that they were only alive to calm Elsie down and coerce her into going along with them without a fuss.

Things had gotten quiet, as if they had settled in for the evening. The mother had become preoccupied brushing Elsie's hair in front of the fireplace, where they were getting warmed up. Elsie seemed to be comforted by the mundane act of brushing her hair, Chris took comfort in the fact that it was calming her down. The two sons were eating whatever they had pulled together from the kitchen.

Supplies had been diminished because the family had prepared to leave and would not be back until spring. Ellen was still in shock, there wasn't a way to comfort her, to get her to snap out of her stupor. They had not tied them up, but they had kept them separated so that they couldn't communicate with each other. The mother didn't want Elsie to be afraid of them, but the boys knew to keep a close eye on the adults, and it was clear that if either of them tried anything, they wouldn't hesitate to take them out.

Would they jump up and leave when they finished eating? Are they on foot, or do they have a car nearby? Do they live nearby? Would they drag them with them, or would they kill them in the cabin? It reminded him of the story told about how the cabin retreat got started.

The original cabin on this plot of land had a less than desirable history. There had been people who were held in a type of bondage on the property, subservient to the landowner. Generations later, the family who inherited the property was ashamed of the abuse that had taken place on the land. It was their desire to change the image that this area projected from its past. They wished for families to come to enjoy the mountain as a place of refuge. A place people could be refreshed and reflect on God and His creation. The land became a retreat. Lots were sold to individuals to build on that could overcome the history, and the rest were cabins used for rental properties.

It was as if the family had read the verse in the Bible that states, "*If My people who are called by My name will humble themselves, and pray and seek My face, and turn from their wicked ways, then I will hear from heaven, and will forgive their sin and heal their land* (2 Chronicles 7:14 NKJV)."

The family would turn over in their graves if they knew what had taken place on the mountain. Killings and now people being held captive once again. It was as if the past was being revisited. Chris was not pleased to be caught up in whatever it was. If they survived this, would they ever be able to come back here? Was this mountain forever cursed with sorrow?

As he watched the boys intensely, he started to imagine how God viewed such people. In his mind right now, they were doomed eternally, for the things that they have done and continue to do. There seemed to be no remorse for their actions.

Yet Chris knew that God sees things differently, he had read many times in Isaiah 55:8,9 (ESV), *"For my thoughts are not your thoughts, neither are your ways my ways, declares the Lord. For as the heavens are higher than the earth, so are my ways higher than your ways and my thoughts than your thoughts."*

Chris was feeling a bit more like Jonah right now, he didn't want to see another path for these people, after witnessing what he had earlier and what they were going through, he thought he wanted them to see God's wrath just like Jonah wanted the wrath to fall on Nineveh.

Although, he had read the Bible enough to know that God sees all sin the same, it's all to be judged. But the beauty in it all is that the Lord shows mercy to all those that call on His name. Therefore, the only difference between him and these men, is the fact that he had accepted Jesus Christ as his Savior, which will keep him from the pit.

Remembering the verses in 1 John 3:15-17 (NKJV), *"Whoever hates his brother is a murderer, and you know that no murderer has eternal life abiding in him. By this we know love, because He laid down His life for us. And we also ought to lay down our lives for the brethren. But whoever has this world's goods, and sees his brother in need, and shuts up his heart from him, how does the love of God abide in him?"* This kind of stung a bit because his heart was not in the right place for these people.

There was a key in the verse from 1 John 3:6 (NKJV) that seemed to be shouting at him. *"Whoever abides in Him does not sin. Whoever sins has neither seen Him nor known Him."* Realizing that these men have never known Jesus. It was being laid on his heart like a heavy anvil, that his assignment was to introduce them to Jesus.

The Apostle Paul's story came to mind from Acts 16, when he was thrust into the inner prison and his feet were put into stocks. Although given an opportunity to be freed, he saw that it was more important to convert the jailer, to save his soul, than to be freed. Chris did not want to be judged for hating another, if he was to follow Jesus' example then he would need to demonstrate love and do his best to get them to know Jesus. Pondering the thought that this act of obedience could make a difference in saving his family. Was this what the Holy Spirit was trying to convey to him? It certainly was wrapped around him like a warm blanket, as if he was to be comforted by this thought.

Unaware of how much time he had left to witness to these people, yet it was clear that sitting quietly didn't seem to accomplish anything. After running things through his head, he decided that the first move should be his. It was best to start a conversation to see if he could decipher some information regarding their motives and whether they knew anything about Jesus and their final destination when they leave this earth.

"So, are you a family?" Chris asked calmly, trying to engage them in conversation.

"What's that to you?" Jasper spouted back aggressively.

"I just wondered if you are related?"

"Yeah, she's, our mom." Zach piped in, not seeing the harm in answering the question.

"I see you have experienced some hard times." Trying to feel them out a little.

"Not as hard as your day." Snickered Zach.

"I'd say we've done pretty good for a day's work, and we didn't have to work so hard at it either." Jasper chuckled getting into the conversation.

"Work, you call killing people work, plundering what is not yours." Shouted Ellen venomously.

That must have hit a nerve and woke her up from her daze. However, she was unaware of what Chris was trying to do. Shock still gripped her, and she was not processing things well, nor thinking clearly. Chris needed to change the subject quickly. To avoid getting them upset, nor did he want to push Ellen over the edge. He was walking a tightrope here, challenged by this new assignment.

"Have you heard of a man called Jesus?"

"I've seen billboards with that man's name on them. I never understood what they were about."

Zach had replied to Chris's question, while Jasper just shook his head in disgust and remained uninterested. The boys could have silenced Chris, but they grew tired of only talking to each other. It wasn't like they made friends wherever they went.

Elsie spoke up. "I know Jesus, Daddy." She was pleased to talk about Jesus.

"Yes, you do, sweetie. And I am happy that you know Him, He will always watch over you."

If anything happened to them, he wanted her to always remember that Jesus was the one that would remain with her. Ellen had done a good job of teaching her about the Bible and the love of Jesus. Chris's thought looking at his precious child was, out of the mouth of babes, they are so innocent and loving.

"We have a friend in Jesus. My mom sings me a song about that."

Elsie was happy to join in the conversation. She liked to have her hair brushed, but this woman didn't seem to know when to stop. Looking in the direction of her mom she could tell she was upset, but she wasn't sure what was really going on with her. It pleased Elsie that her daddy was talking about Jesus, a subject she liked to hear about, and one that she knew more about than even her parents were aware of.

Jesus visits her on Fridays for tea and she had visited Him in Heaven on a special occasion. Between the two of them, they had wonderful conversations about Heaven. And Jesus revealed to her, that when she got older, she would have a special assignment. Not sure what that meant, but it sounded good if He referred to it as special. Talking with Jesus and being in His presence was her favorite thing to do, there was never the presence of fear or worries, time always seemed to slip by. Her parents knew about her tea parties, but they hadn't realized how real they were.

Turning his attention back to Zach. "Maybe I should ask, do you recognize God as the Creator of all things? *'For by Him all things were created, both in the heavens and on earth, visible and invisible, whether thrones or dominions or rulers or authorities—all things have been created through Him and for Him. He is before all things, and in Him all things hold together* (Colossians1:16,17 NASB).'"

"Well, I understand him to be the Judge from above, that condemns us." Barked Zach as if he didn't like the idea of being judged.

"He is going to condemn you all, for what you have done." Snapped Ellen, breaking her silence once again. Chris looked in her direction with a stare that said, stand down. She was confused and silenced by his look, withdrawing inside herself for a while to try and cope with the trauma experienced.

"There's that feisty woman I saw earlier." Jasper stated with a smile that unnerved Chris.

Chris tried again, desperately wanting to get back on target. "God is love, it is not His desire to see any perish or to be tormented. 1 John 4:16 (NASB) states, '*We have come to know and have believed the love which God has for us. God is love, and the one who abides in love abides in God, and God abides in him.*'"

"You said so yourself, you got to know Him to be loved. I'm sure he has no love for us." Zach stated with some remorse in his voice, indicating that there was regret for his actions.

Jasper spouted off, "You ain't loved by nobody, except maybe ma, and I'm not sure she even cares about you. Look at her over there with that little girl. She must have wanted you to be a little girl."

Zach threw his cup at Jasper, which got a rise out of his mother. Distracted by their actions, she yelled at them both to settle down, it was clear she didn't want anything to upset Elsie. The hair brushing continued while humming a tune.

The boys thought she had lost her mind, yet she was plotting how she was going to secure Elsie's confidence at the same time as getting rid of her parents. There was no way she was going to lug those two around just to keep the child happy. She could be quite cunning and very dangerous, which is what kept the boys in line.

Chris plugged along trying to keep Zach engaged in conversation. "I believe God loves all humanity. I believe we all came from God the Father when we were conceived, and if we came from the Father then we are loved. You may have fallen, but you are not forgotten. He desires for your return to Him, and the only way to the Father is through Jesus Christ."

Jasper couldn't resist the remark that would poke fun at Zach. "The only father you came from is a dead thief. This man is filling your head with a bunch of nonsense."

Zach ignored Jasper, now that he was a little curious about what Chris was talking about. "So, who is this Jesus and why does He have the only access?"

Zach was showing interest and that is what Chris was desiring. "Jesus is the Son of God, '*Being found in appearance as a man, He humbled Himself by becoming obedient to the point of death, even death on a cross.*

For this reason also, God highly exalted Him, and bestowed on Him the name which is above every name, so that at the name of Jesus EVERY KNEE WILL BOW, of those who are in heaven and on earth and under the earth (Philippians 2:8-10 NASB).' It's written that, '*He was manifested to take away our sins, and in Him there is no sin* (1 John 3:5 NKJV).'"

"Are you saying that He never did anything wrong?" This was a statement that was hard to believe.

"Well, now you know he is lying, ain't nobody that good." Jasper still poking fun at Zach for wasting his time on lies.

"Exactly. Yet, He is spotless, unlike man because He is divine. '*The LORD saw that the wickedness of man was great in the earth, and that every intent of the thoughts of his heart was only evil continually* (Genesis 6:5 NKJV).' I guess things haven't really changed much from the beginning of creation. But God provided a way to save us from ourselves. Don't get me wrong, the Bible tells us that '*The face of the LORD is against those who do evil* (1 Peter 3:12 NKJV).'"

Straightening himself up in the chair drawing Zach into what he was saying. "He does not align Himself with darkness because He is Holy. Yet God sent His Son to die in our place, so that we may have access to God the Father in heaven. You see, sin is a death sentence, God provided a solution for the problem of man's sin. Jesus dying on the cross satisfied the judgement of the sin we commit. '*For all have sinned and fall short of the glory of God* (Romans 3:23 NKJV).' It is stated in Romans 5:6 (NKJV), '*For when we were still without strength, in due time Christ died for the ungodly.*'"

"We fell a long time ago and I don't see change in our future." Zach said with some degree of regret.

"Jesus endured much for us, it's through His sacrifice and demonstration of grace that we are made righteous before God. In other words, He erases our wrongs and accepts us, if we accept Him."

"It's too late for any higher Being to find any good in us." Zach was frustrated now. A distinct feeling of being very lost, figuring it was too late for him and any of his family.

"It's stated in Romans 6:23 (NKJV), '*For the wages of sin is death, but the gift of God is eternal life in Christ Jesus our Lord.*' It's a gift that is there for all, if we turn to God and repent and recognize His Son for what He has done for us. As stated in 1 John 1:9 (NKJV), '*If we confess our sins, he is faithful and just to forgive us our sins and to cleanse us from all unrighteousness.'"*

"What does repent mean? That sounds like a fancy word." Zach asking questions was a good sign.

"It means you've got to stop being evil, pure evil." Ellen said with a piercing tone, waking from her trance. "Have you never heard that, *'Bad Company corrupts good morals* (1 Corinthians 15:33 NASB).' Excuse me, apparently, ya'll don't have any morals."

Well, Chris knew now that she was awake over there, but apparently, she still wasn't aware of what he was doing. He continued to talk to keep Zach interested and to silence Ellen's temper before it got them in more trouble.

At this point, Jasper was ignoring most of what was being said, likely because he was confused about the topic, too entrenched in his evil ways. However, his eyes were focused only on Ellen. Chris assumed the mother was caught up in her own fantasy world over there still pampering Elsie, like some kind of plaything. Evidently, she wasn't following the conversation. What Chris was unaware of was that she was scheming his death.

Chris continued with an explanation. "It means to turn from your ways and thoughts and follow God's path for you."

"Like some path down the yellow brick road?" Now twisting the narrative, projecting it as a mythical unattainable path.

"Not exactly, it's a new direction for your life. Once you recognize you need Jesus and accept Him as your Lord and Savior, the Holy Spirit will guide you. It's important to know that you should not *'be deceived and deluded and misled; God will not allow Himself to be sneered at (scorned, disdained, or mocked by mere pretensions or professions, or by His precepts being set aside.) [He inevitably deludes himself who attempts to delude God.] For whatever a man sows, that and that only is what he will reap. For he who sows to his own flesh (lower nature, sensuality) will from the flesh reap decay and ruin and destruction, but he who sows to the Spirit will from the Spirit reap eternal life* (Galatians 6:7,8 AMP).'"

"I don't think I need anyone; I'm doing just fine on my own." Zach stated firmly to throw off his brother.

Zach could tell Jasper was getting frustrated with him, and ma didn't look so happy either. He was confused about a lot of things, but he knew what his family was doing was wrong. It had always been made clear that if he tried to leave them, they would kill him. It wasn't so much that blood was thicker than water, as it was the shedding of his own blood, that they would surely do, which kept him captive.

Not understanding the fear that Zach was ensnared in, Chris moved forward engaging him further in conversation.

"That's where you are wrong. We all need someone. Just so happens that it's something we have in common, we've all sinned, we all need forgiveness, and we all need Jesus. If you are unable to hear and receive the gift He has for you, then you will remain lost. And as the Word in John 8:44 (NKJV) says, *'You are of your father the devil, and the desires of your father you want to do. He was a murderer from the beginning, and does not stand in the truth, because there is no truth in him. When he speaks a lie, he speaks from his own resources, for he is a liar and the father of it.'"*

"I can vouch that our father was surely a devil. Ma put an end to him." Zach stated, letting a little of their history slip.

"Don't listen to this guy, we have each other. We've always had each other's back. Where one goes, we all go." Jasper pointing out their so-called brotherhood.

"And I can only hope that it's to jail for all the crimes that you have committed." Ellen was still getting her two cents in.

If she wasn't careful, they might muzzle her. Or worse, they might shut her up permanently. It was as if she didn't care what they did to her, she wasn't thinking clearly. Chris was starting to think she had a death wish. Was she so depressed that she couldn't see what he was doing?

"John 10:10 (NKJV) states, *'The thief does not come except to steal, and to kill, and to destroy. I have come that they may have life and that they may have it more abundantly.'* Jesus wants to improve your life here, and to give you eternal life. Look, the Gospel means good news, it's what Jesus wanted us to share with the world. It's a message of reversal. Reversing a curse and turning it into a blessing."

"Well, you had the first part of that right, we come to steal, kill, and leave destruction in our path."

"I realize I'm throwing a lot of information out that may not make sense to you right now, but I think it's worth thinking about. *'What man is there among you who, if his son asks for bread, will give him a stone? Or if he asks for a fish, will he give him a serpent? If you then, being evil, know how to give good gifts to your children, how much more will your Father who is in heaven give good things to those who ask Him! Therefore, whatever you want men to do to you, do also to them, for this is the Law and the Prophet* (Matthew 7:9-12 NKJV)."

"You sound like some kind of preacher going on like that." Zach didn't really like being preached at, it felt like some kind of condemnation.

"Not a preacher, just a Believer who trusts in the Lord."

Elsie had been listening intently to what her father was saying, not understanding it all but getting the gist of it. What really caught her attention and made her eyes light up was that Jesus was in the room with them. He was smiling at her dad, which pleased her. She wanted to run to Him and hug Him, but He had motioned that she was to remain quiet and let her father do his best to talk to these men.

The smugness of these men became too much for Ellen, it was repugnant to her and reminded her of Haman in the story of Esther in the Bible. The concept of Haman's noose was pleasing her right about now. How she'd love the tables to turn on these cruel people. She wanted a reversal to happen to these culprits that were holding them captive, that had shot her dad.

Remembering the verses in her head, *"On the day that the enemies of the Jews had hoped to overpower them, the opposite occurred, in that the Jews themselves overpowered those who hated them* (Esther 9:1 NKJV)." With God on their side nothing was impossible. A plan just needed to be devised to overcome them.

The ridiculing brother Jasper spoke up. "Zach, you need to get your head out of the clouds over there. You aren't going anywhere near a puffy lifestyle, up in the clouds floating around like some little angel."

"Your only destination is eternal torment." Spouted Ellen with disgust.

"Oh, mommy, don't say that. Jesus says he doesn't want anyone to go there. Father God wants us all to come home." Elsie said sweetly.

"You're right, honey, Jesus will decide where they go, not me."

"And you don't float around in heaven either. It's a beautiful place that God created." Elsie was correcting Jasper.

All eyes went to spunky little Elsie. "And just how do you know all that, little one?"

"Jesus has taken me there." Answering simply and matter-of-factly.

She looked in Jesus's direction who had beckoned her to step lightly, but she was speaking truth so how could that be silenced?

"What did you say, dear?" Louise finally joined the conversation now that Elsie was involved.

"That Jesus took me to heaven, for a visit. He comes to have tea every Friday with me, and I asked to see heaven, so He took me there, so that I could see where He was from."

"And what did you do there?" Jasper asked, almost mocking her.

"We had tea." Elsie stated, thinking that was a silly question.

"Where did you have tea? In his house?" Louise was asking with a worried tone.

Louise was starting to think the child was touched. Maybe taking her on would be more of a challenge than she was expecting. But then again, maybe she could correct this behavior that her parents had encouraged. Her parents were aware of her tea parties, but they had never heard her talk like this before, about heaven. All were assuming she had quite the imagination.

"No, in a pretty garden where the animals talked to me. There are many beautiful houses there, but mine is not built yet." No one was ready for what she was sharing.

Louise and the boys cracked up laughing at her. They couldn't believe the nonsense she was creating out of thin air. At this point, Louise's thoughts were what on earth have these people been teaching this child. She decided it was the parent's fault that she was deranged.

When Chris came to his daughter's defense, explaining she had a great imagination, she could be sharing a dream she had. Elsie was confused by the boys laughing at her and more so by her father's remarks.

"Daddy, I really went to heaven with Jesus. I didn't dream that. I was awake." She was defiant and adamant about that fact.

"Things seem real in a dream, honey."

"I didn't dream it. Just like I know Jesus is with us, right now."

"Jesus is always with us." Confirming that statement based on Scripture.

"I know that, but He is in the room, with us."

They all looked around the room as if they were going to see something. Jasper looked a little afraid, like he was going to see some sort of ghost or some sort of apparition. The others looked back at Elsie to see what else she would say about Jesus being in the room, now a little scared. Chris was showing concern for Elsie, had she been traumatized by the events of the day.

"Jesus is very proud of you, Daddy."

Chris smiled back at Elsie, not sure what was happening, but he was becoming more concerned, first his wife and now his daughter. The trauma was just too much for them.

"You didn't tell us your daughter has lost her mind." Jasper stated gruffly.

Zach was shaking his head as if he had no idea what was going on, things were seeming to be a little out of control and here he thought his family had problems.

Louise asked in a harsh tone. "What have you been teaching this child?"

Figuring she had her work cut out for her, to undo the damage that Elsie had been put through with these people's teachings.

"She's perfectly sane. And we teach her what the Bible says. You people need to read the Bible. First and foremost, nothing is impossible for God." Ellen was emphatic with her words coming to the aid of her daughter.

Looking in Chris' direction, realizing he was even doubting his own daughters' words. She hadn't heard her say any of this before, but there was no reason to doubt her. Elsie had heard the stories and knew something about what she was talking about. Ellen continued talking hoping to get through to Chris, more than these three, that don't know anything about the Bible.

"Do we not teach, that the story's in the Bible are real events that occurred? We don't get to pick and choose what we want to believe, it's a matter of facts and God's written Word is true."

Glaring directly at her husband. "Did Paul not say that he was taken to the third Heaven, and John was taken to the throne room. What about Elijah in 2 Kings (2:11), being taken up to heaven by a whirlwind. He didn't die nor did Enoch, who walked with God (Genesis 5:24). It's even suggested that Moses was taken by God in Deuteronomy (34:5-6)."

"That's true." Chris was processing what was being said.

"In Revelation 11:12 (NKJV), '*They heard a loud voice from heaven saying to them, 'Come up here.' And they ascended to heaven in a cloud, and their enemies saw them.*' They went up and were seen going up. And what about places being prepared for us, such as the ones spoken of in Hebrews (11:16 NASB), '*They desire a better country, that is, a heavenly one. Therefore, God is not ashamed to be called their God; for He has prepared a city for them.*'"

She was awake and on a roll, preaching to her own husband. "And let's not forget John 14:2 (NIV), '*My Father's house has many rooms; if that were not so, would I have told you that I am going there to prepare a place for you?*' It's our inheritance that He prepares for us, and we are prepared for. Remember the Word in 1 Peter (1:4,5 NKJV), '*An inheritance incorruptible and undefiled and that does not fade away, reserved in heaven for you, who are kept by the power of God through faith for salvation ready to be revealed in the last time.*' Our baby girl is not a lunatic, she is gifted. The Word is truth to her, if she says she sees Jesus, then we should be so lucky."

She was directing her words to Chris with power and influence. It was certain that the Holy Spirit was with her to guide her to each verse she needed to recall for such a time as this. Even she would have to take time to allow this message to resonate with herself.

Louise was convinced that they were all off their rocker. More reason for her to save this child from them. As she sat there quietly, she had devised a plan to bring this child up in their family, to have her marry Zach, and birth her a grandchild to raise. This would perpetuate the next generation of Cassidy's. Elsie was young but would be raised by her and would be a young bride for Zach, who was now seventeen and would make a good husband. She saw their future all laid out. It was just a matter of time.

Song "Soul Worth Saving" by Apollo LTD

3

REFUGE

Pop avoided the bullet by dropping to the ground. The timing had been perfect, it appeared as if he had been shot. He had remained still long enough to realize they were not coming after him. Apparently, they thought he was hit and were uninterested in checking on him. He stayed low doing his best at an army crawl down the hill, until he thought it was safe for him to rise and run.

It had crossed his mind to go back to the cabin and see if he could help them somehow, but then he thought better of that plan, because he had no weapon and no phone available to him. The best plan at the moment, was to seek shelter, to make sure he wasn't followed, then to find help from someone else close by, preferably someone with a means to contact the police.

Coming upon the first cabin he crossed, he found that it was empty. Relieved not to have discovered a dead body yet hoping that he would have found someone with a cell phone. He had been running in the opposite direction of the car parking area. Which was located out the front of their cabin. However, he had been shot at out the back side of the cabin, therefore he fled in that direction. It may have been a better plan to circle around at a lower elevation from their cabin, but he ran the risk of running into the thugs. He was headed as far away from them as he could be, in order to seek help.

Between the shock of being shot at, the army crawl through the woods, then the run, and now the fear for his family, he was exhausted by the time

25

he broke into the cabin. Dehydration can cause muscle cramping as well as high blood pressure, after all he was an older man. Water was needed and the cabin could provide that, there was no need for him to drop dead in the woods, accomplishing nothing.

Although he didn't want to waste any time, he knew what was at stake. After getting his fill of water he sat down and listened intently for any activity going on outside the cabin. He hadn't heard any other gunshots, nor anyone traipsing through the woods. It was now clear that no one was following him.

The exhaustion got to him; his legs were now cramping, making it difficult to maneuver. Things were starting to look a little bleaker.

Realizing things were about to get even more difficult for him, the sun was starting to set. This was going to present a huge problem. He knew these woods pretty well, but finding his way in the dark was another matter altogether, especially now when it was more difficult for him to move around. The mountain not only gets really dark at night, with little light to guide you, but when the sun goes down, it gets really cold, not to mention predators roam at night. However, George was aware of the predators that his family was facing, and it gave him the courage to continue on.

Reflecting on his situation he turned to God and His Word, "*Turn to me and be gracious to me, For I am lonely and afflicted. The troubles of my heart are enlarged; Bring me out of my distresses. Look upon my affliction and my trouble, And forgive all my sins. Look upon my enemies, for they are many, And they hate me with violent hatred. Guard my soul and deliver me; Do not let me be ashamed, for I take refuge in You* (Psalm 25:16-20 NASB)."

Taking a blanket from one of the beds in the cabin, he wrapped up in it, and headed out, while there was still some dim light left. It was clear now that he was not being followed, but he wasn't going to dawdle either, his family's lives were at stake and that burdened his heart. He needed to move as fast as his body would allow him to move. Lifting prayers for his family's safety with every step he took. As he moved forward through the night Psalm 91 (NIV) came to him and he found some comfort.

"*Whoever dwells in the shelter of the Most High will rest in the shadow of the Almighty. I will say of the LORD, 'He is my refuge and my fortress, my God, in whom I trust.' Surely he will save you from the fowler's snare and from the deadly pestilence. He will cover you with his feathers, and under his wings you will find refuge; his faithfulness will be your shield and rampart. You will not fear the terror of night, nor the arrow that flies by day, nor the pestilence that stalks in the darkness, nor the plague that destroys at midday. A thousand may fall at your side, ten thousand at your right hand, but it will not come near you. You will only observe with your eyes and see the punishment of the wicked.*

If you say, 'The LORD is my refuge,' and you make the Most High your dwelling, no harm will overtake you, no disaster will come near your tent. For he will command his angels concerning you to guard you in all your ways; they will lift you up in their hands, so that you will not strike your foot against a stone. You will tread on the lion and the cobra; you will trample the great lion and the serpent.

'Because he loves me,' says the LORD, 'I will rescue him; I will protect him, for he acknowledges my name. He will call on me, and I will answer him; I will be with him in trouble, I will deliver him and honor him. With long life I will satisfy him and show him my salvation.'"

These verses Pop knew by heart. They were his favorite and had always been a great comfort to him. They were never more appropriate than right now. The Lord protected him from the bullet, helped him find refuge in the cabin where he needed rest and water to carry on this courageous journey. The night would not terrorize him knowing that the Lord and His angels were watching over him and shoring up his footing, which were needed. His eyes were adjusting enough to prevent him from falling into a ravine.

His family was counting on him to bring help. He prayed that no disaster would come to his family back at the cabin. The Lord is there in his time of trouble and will deliver them all from this evil.

Reciting John 8:12 (NASB) with each step taken. "*I am the Light of the world; he who follows Me will not walk in the darkness, but will have the Light of life.'*"

The night sky continued to darken, and it was getting harder for him to see where he was headed. When suddenly at a distance he could see a light appear, as if it were a beacon directing him. He just kept moving in the direction of the light in hopes that it would bring him aid. His refuge was just over the hill.

The more he focused on the light, he was reminded of a poem that he had heard as a young man by Phil Soar, called "A Beacon Of Light".

He tried to recall the words of the poem, missing a stanza or two as he struggled forward, his memory a bit fuzzy or was it because he was so tired, but with each line he was brought a little more comfort.

> "The beacon shone atop the hill
> A fire so bright, the world stood still
> And viewed from many miles away
> It burned by night and flickered by day
>
> They prayed for peace and watched the flames
> That danced in sync whilst ash remained
> And where the light shined brighter still
> They all looked up toward that hill"

As he approached the house with the lights on, he hoped that he didn't startle them. He would hate to be running from a threat only to walk into a bullet, seeking help. Knocking at the door with some urgency, the front porch lights came on, an elderly woman came to the door, slightly cracking it open leaving the chain latched, she asked in a strong inquisitive voice.

"What do you want?"

Leery of intruders and shocked to have visitors late at night, especially one that was cloaked in a blanket. It was considered bravery to have even gone to the door.

"I need help. Do you have a phone that I could use to call the police?"

"Where is your phone?" She asked confused by the request.

"I am without my phone, that's why I need to borrow yours." George was trying to be patient, but he was getting worried about his family, and he was now so close to getting them some help.

"I'm going to call the police if you don't leave." She was threatening.

"Please, please do call the police, right away."

"Am I in danger?"

"No, but my family is in danger, and I need the police." This just wasn't making sense to her.

"Why do you have a blanket wrapped around you? Are you concealing something from me? You aren't some kind of flasher, are you?"

She was a woman with a lot of questions. Pop was just wanting to get the attention of the police, and he was desperate to make that call, but she was more interested in what he had wrapped around him. Why on earth would she think that an old man would want to be flashing anyone on a cold night? He started to wonder if she had a car, he'd hotwire it if he had to, and drive to the police station, himself. Only he realized that would take longer than making a call.

"I'd appreciate your assistance if you could just call the police. I am wrapped in a blanket because it's cold out here, and I have been wandering through the woods looking for someone to help me."

"I agree, it's been getting colder every night this week. Would you like some hot cocoa?"

"That would be very nice. But it really is urgent that you call the police."

Pop was getting even more frustrated but tried to show patience so as not to scare her in any way. She was after all, his refuge in his time of need, and key to saving his family.

Securing the door, she walked away. He had no idea if she would call the police first or make the hot cocoa. But she left him out in the cold. It was only a moment or so when he heard her talking to someone. Was someone else there or was she talking on the phone? Then she came back to the door and shoved the phone at him.

"They want to talk to you. I forgot to ask you your name."

"George Johnson." He said firmly, as he took the phone and spoke to the policeman on the other end.

Starting his explanation that he had witnessed someone getting shot, back at The Cabins, and he himself had been shot at but was able to get away. How his family was in grave danger, being held hostage at his cabin. Giving the address and wanting them to head that way promptly. Stating that he had no idea if they were dead or alive.

Miss Mae was overhearing all that was said and became even more frightened, yet less afraid of George. She brought him a cup of hot cocoa but didn't open the door fully. He thanked her and warmed his hands with the cup before drinking the warm beverage. A blanket was pushed through the partially opened door, shortly after.

"Maybe that will help," she said hesitantly.

Knowing that it was cold and that he was stressed, she may have felt bad for him, but it was best to wait on the police before opening the door to him. It was clear that George was no threat to her, but she was still afraid.

Living alone was difficult for an aging woman, and she had to be cautious, it's how she survived this long on her own, along with her faith in the Lord. 1 Timothy 5:5 (NASB) wasn't wasted on her; she knew it well. *"Now she who is a widow indeed and who has been left alone, has fixed her hope on God and continues in entreaties and prayers night and day."*

Prayers had been lifted earlier from Miss Mae to help her overcome loneliness. Although the situation was not the same in the Bible, the words rang true for her in Psalm 38:8-10 (NIV). *"I am feeble and utterly crushed; I groan in anguish of heart, All my longings lie open before you, Lord; my sighing is not hidden from you. My heart pounds, my strength fails me; even the light has gone from my eyes."* She longed for company and God had been good to her, He brought her someone to talk to before she had done something that she may have regretted.

Nighttime was the worst time to feel the pang of loneliness. And the nights came earlier in the fall with little evidence of life around her. It could look quite desolate in the mountains during winter, which was at her doorstep. She was now presented with a guest on her front porch and the police would be visiting soon as well. God had brought her a lot of activity and excitement into her life all at once, although it may not have been the exhilaration she was looking for.

The local police knew Miss Mae well and where she lived. She had grown up on the farm and remained at the homestead after the rest of the family had long been gone. It was not unusual for Miss Mae to call in a police complaint, on some lonely afternoons to drum up some kind of excuse for the police to drop by for a visit. A typical call might be that her chickens got loose, and she needed help rounding them up, assuming someone had vandalized the chicken coop.

It could be expected by the officers that she'd give them a short grocery list of items to stop and pick up for her on their way out. When they arrived, there was always a fresh pie or cake right from the oven with homemade sweet tea ready for them. It was rather like a reward for making the grocery store stop for her. The officers always enjoyed her baked treats.

A call in the evening was unlike Miss Mae, so they knew something was wrong. Alerted to the fear in her voice, they were headed in her direction as a high priority to check on her, and to talk further with George about the threat that they could be walking into.

The local police were not used to this kind of trouble on the mountain, so they wanted to call in some support from the Sheriff's department. The police had informed George over the phone that there had been no reports of gunfire in the area, which was now a greater concern to George. How many people had they shot to keep things quiet? It may take the Sheriff a little longer to get there, but the local police would compile the information needed from George to set up their approach to the cabin. George just wanted them to take some kind of action as soon as they could.

Miss Mae proceeded to talk to George from the door. "I'm sorry to hear about your family. I know you are worried."

"Yes, very worried. I'm afraid all this is taking too long." He was exasperated.

"You said your name is, George?" Miss Mae was just trying to create some chitchat.

"George Johnson, the kids call me Pop."

"That's sweet. How many kids do you have."

"My wife and I have the one daughter, Ellen, who is married now to a fine young man, Chris Chaplain. They have a beautiful little girl named, Elsie."

"As in the cow," she asked inquisitively, holding back a giggle.

"I never thought about it that way. She just looks like an Elsie, always been our little Elsie. The light of my life."

"How old is she?"

"Four going on fifteen. She's smart as a whip." He stated proudly.

"Are you all renting at The Cabins?"

"No, we are among the few that purchased property and built our own cabin years ago, when Ellen was just a little girl."

"So, is your wife with the kids?"

"No, my wife went to be with the Lord several years ago. She is greatly missed."

There was a sense of sadness in his tone. One that Miss Mae could relate to.

"I'm sorry to hear that."

They continued to talk and before too long the local police showed up and they all went inside where Miss Mae was trying to get everyone a hot beverage. Apologizing that she didn't have a hot cake ready for them, but there was yesterday's pound cake ready to be served up. It was important to be hospitable to her guests. The officers were doting on her and making sure she was alright. She knew them all by name and thanked them for their concern for her. It was clear that she was pleased to have all this company in the evening, it would surely help her pass the long hours of the night. Making it through one more day.

The police turned their attention to George for questioning, regarding what he saw and experienced, searching for more details. He was a little frustrated with them because he felt like he had already given them information over the phone, he was expecting them to be reacting to the threat his family was under. Although going over the information again, more was revealed. The time of day the shooting took place, its exact location, the movements of the two shooters, and that a woman was with them.

Questions were asked about the cabin's set up, entry points were key. They were forwarding the information to the Sheriff's department, so they could be brought up to speed, as well as working on some searches in the database. George wanted them to act right away, he felt their hesitancy and wasn't pleased. He would have just preferred to be armed and headed back to the cabin himself. Although it did make sense to know as much detail as possible before rushing into a situation that might cause more harm than good all the way around.

After conveying the information back and forth, the Sheriff decided they'd head straight to the cabin, sensing the clear and present danger the family was in. However, it was insisted that additional help be called in, this may be larger than they think after hearing the report of a rash of killings and looting taking place all the way down from Tennessee. Terror had made its way into their little community.

Apparently, there had been some survivors, who were able to describe them, as a woman and two younger men traveling together looting homes and shooting witnesses. Sounded like the same MO as what George had just described.

Upon further investigating from the station, the identities of the three came through. There was Louise Cassidy, age forty-two, her son Jasper, age twenty-seven, and another by the name of Zach Cassidy, age seventeen. They were from the hills of Tennessee with a rap sheet as long as your arm. They had been able to evade the police for over a year because they kept moving about, but they were now up on charges of multiple homicides. This was going to be a huge case.

The strange thing coming from the reports was the fact that there were witnesses that survived. All three were considered marksmen and yet people were able to escape. One report stated that he felt like the kid missed him on purpose. When he had fallen to the ground and froze in place, they all moved on. When Pop heard that report, it started to make sense why they didn't come after him and why he had evaded a bullet.

Song "Brighter Days" by Blessing Offor

4

THE FAMILY

More history was being revealed about the Cassidy family over the radio as they were moving into position. It was always best to know as much as possible about the people you were trying to take into custody when a shoot-out may take place. It was better to try to get into their heads.

The mountains of Tennessee is where they called home, before they left on their murderess spree. Deep in the hills distant from the rest of society, the Cassidy's lived out their lives on their own terms. Never interacting much with many around them, therefore keeping to themselves and to the mountain. Occasionally other family members would come by to trade with them, and give them news of other family members, as well as what was happening in the world.

Living off the land honed their skills in marksmanship. As soon as you could hold onto a rifle you were taught how to use it. If you were to eat, you had to be able to catch it. It was a very sheltered and difficult life; yet it was all that the family had known. Louise's father was raised that way, and he had planned to raise his family after the same model.

There was a knowledge of God, the Creator. Even if they had never heard the words in a Bible or the name of Jesus spoken, they were aware of a higher Being that brought rain for the crops and provided meat through the provision of small animals. They witnessed the beauty of a rainbow, and the majesty of a sunset, it was apparent that someone, something bigger than them was in control.

There were certain commands handed down through family members, but they didn't recognize them as verses from the Bible, just words that they were to live by. *"Children, obey your parents in the Lord, for this is right. 'Honor Your Father and mother' —which is the first commandment with a promise—so that it may go well with you and that you may enjoy long life on the earth* (Ephesians 6:1-3 NIV)."

Louise had been the unfortunate girl child born into the family, which meant more abuse by the family, however, she didn't know anything different. She was told it was for her good and informed her that it was an act of love. The power of one's words was clear to them all. Words were wielded like a sword in their family. They could cut you down to nothing or they could encourage you to push forward, there wasn't a lot of building up going on, for fear someone would break ranks. Mostly words of control.

The emphasis from her father was the importance to carry on the family name. Therefore, at age thirteen, she had been given to her older brother, Sam, as his bride, in order to procreate a family, and keep the family name going. They didn't follow the laws of the land, being hidden on the mountaintop, and there was no one to tell her what they were doing was wrong.

Louise gave birth to Jasper by the time she turned fifteen and raised him the best she knew how. There were no maternal influences around considering her mother had died when she was young, it would have to come instinctively. There had been many miscarriages, making Jasper even more of a treasure to the family. They were unaware of the problems with genetics and blood types, how incest caused miscarriages. Respecting your elders was something that was institutionalized, it was their element of control, used by her father and something she learned to wield herself with her boys.

When a cousin, Kyle, had come by to trade with her father, he had shown an interest in Louise. She had blossomed into a beautiful young woman, that could have captured any young man's attention. He showed her compassion and respect, something she had never experienced. A spark had developed between them, and she enjoyed his visits more and more. It was his mistake to have come around as frequently as he did, which became suspicious, and ultimately resulted in his death. It didn't matter if there was anything going on, or not, if her husband suspected something, he had the right to deal with it, as he saw fit. It was the law of the mountain.

Louise was devastated upon hearing of Kyle's death. It had been her only glimpse of happiness, until Zach was born into the family. She was able to carry this baby to full term, which she was grateful for. Zach looked a lot like Kyle, she was secretly glad of that fact, but it was something she kept to herself, aware that she had to worry for his safety.

Having heard somewhere that a baby always looked like the daddy at birth, for the daddy to be able to recognize that he was the father. With that knowledge she kept Zach wrapped and shielded from Sam, so that he would not suspect anything and try to harm the baby. Afterall, Zach was still a Cassidy and should be protected. It was a relief to her at the time, that it was another boy child. It was thought that her boys would grow up and protect her from the rest of the family, she had grown weary of the abuse.

Secretly, she always wanted a girl child, although she didn't want one to grow up under the conditions she had to grow up with. Experiencing the kindness from Kyle, taught her that life could be better than what she was living. He had spoken of things outside the mountain lifestyle which piqued her interest. Kyle had shown love towards Louise and wanted to take her away from the family and all the abuse. She would have left with him had it not been for his untimely death.

Once her father died, she found the strength to kill her husband, to get free from Sam's abuse. She was free to leave the mountain with her boys. Nothing was holding her back now, except law and order which she knew little of. It was only taught that you fight for what you need to survive. Life had been hard for her, and a change was needed. She was ready to take what she wanted to live outside the mountain life. She did not worry, nor feared any consequences. In her mind she had lived in captivity, and nothing could be worse than what she had just freed herself from.

Jasper had always been given everything he wanted, as far as the code of the mountain would allow and was treated like the treasure that the family saw him as, for he was the one to carry on the family name. He was allowed to go to town, where he witnessed people living a different way, he wanted some of that lifestyle, yet he had been held to the mountain as well, as long as his grandfather was alive, he would have to live on the mountain.

Through trips to town, he felt some freedom and had an opportunity to feel like a man on his own. He had been with several women of the town but had not selected one as a wife. His father was encouraging him to make a choice, and he would handle the rest. But a selection was never made. He felt like that would tie him to the mountain even more and he had bigger plans.

When Jasper witnessed his mother kill his father with a shotgun, shock rose within him, but then a sigh of relief. It was a flash of freedom that crossed his mind, but he knew not to cross his mother, she was the power broker now. So, when his mother decided to leave the mountain, he was fine with it. Ready to start a new life. To him, he was clearing a path to his own freedom, possibly freedom from the family all together. If he killed people, it was because they were getting in the way of his destiny. He was used to killing things that provided something for him, people were no different.

Louise looked at Zach as her ray of hope, remembering what could have been with Kyle. It was never shared with him that he had a different daddy than Jasper. If Sam had ever caught wind of that he might have killed Zach, and even turned-on Louise. She had not given him the number of children he wanted. There were times that she feared for her life, because he would get so upset about it, claiming he was going to take another wife. But as long as her father was alive, she was safe.

Sam had taken Zach to town a few times to demonstrate to him how they conducted purchasing supplies and trading with some of the locals. Once he had gotten old enough to start looking for a bride of his own, Sam took him into town more frequently. Jasper had not selected a bride, and it was felt that the family needed to start growing.

There had been encouragement for Zach to look around at the young fillies, as Sam called the young ladies in town, as if he was shopping for a horse. There really wasn't many to choose from and there was a lack of interest on Zach's part, they were too old or too young. Zach was never clear about how he was going to get to know any of them personally, considering the fact he never got free time from the mountain or family. That was never discussed between them, and now they were thrown on another path, altogether.

Zach always felt like he was different from the rest of the family. He killed to eat, but he was not a killer. It never felt right to take a life for no reason, but he wasn't going to challenge his family. If killing was for his protection he understood it, self-preservation. The killing spree that they found themselves a part of was not a lifestyle that Zach wanted a part in.

Knowing if he tried to run, like these innocent people, he would be shot as well. The best he could do was to shoot, and miss, and hope that the people would fall to the ground and freeze, while he would divert Jasper's attention, allowing the victims to escape and the ability for the Cassidy family to walk away.

In a few cases, he had to shoot and wound people to get them to fall. But it was not his intent to kill. Witnesses would later share how Zach would cover for their escape. In some instances, he would shoot into the wall and instruct them to lay still until they were gone, he'd shut the door behind him, and not discuss what happened, he just encouraged his family to move on. Jasper just assumed Zach did as he was told.

Song "Come As You Are" by Crowder

5

OPPORTUNITY

Jasper had nodded off briefly, while Louise was playing a game with Elsie to further capture her trust through an attempt to spoil her with anything she wanted. Elsie was thirsty and hungry; Louise was happy to supply her with whatever she could find in the kitchen. She was determined that she was going to raise this little girl as her own, and that Elsie was going to make a perfect bride for Zach. Although, she would have to cleanse her from the brainwashing she felt her parents had put her through. This child thinks she sees a man that is not there, how bizarre is that. Time with her would correct that.

Chris wanted to share a story with Zach regarding courage to do what you know is right. Quoting Luke 1:37 (NKJV) to get his attention.

"'*For with God nothing will be impossible.*' One must align themself with the Creator of all things."

He started telling him of a story in the Bible, how Daniel and his people were taken captive, yet they didn't give up on their faith, they found the courage to refuse mandates that were handed down to bow and worship the King versus their God. Explaining that they had been taught to never do anything that conflicts with Gods moral and ethical principles.

Chris continued to share how God saved these people amid adversity, and how they stood strong knowing they would face consequences. Trying to make the point how it was more important to do the right thing than to live a lie. Sharing that there were three men in this story who refused to bow to the King, who were sentenced to a fiery furnace. The furnace had been turned up so high that the guards dropped dead trying to get them to the opening, yet after being thrown into the fire, the three men were walking around with a fourth man unscathed.

He recited Isaiah 43:2,3 (NKJV). "'*When you walk through the fire, you shall not be burned, Nor shall the flame scorch you. For I am the LORD your God, The Holy One of Israel, your Savior.*'"

"Who was the fourth man, and how did he get in the fire with them?"

"The fourth man was Jesus, their Savior. He showed up during their time of need, His opportunity to save them and witness to others. This was due to their faith and ability to trust God. Another one of those men, Daniel, whom the King admired, also had been unjustly charged for his faith. He was thrown into the Lion's den and survived because God shut the mouths of the lions. A demonstration of God's power. God protects according to His will and purposes."

"Maybe those lions weren't hungry." Zach retorted.

"No, they devoured the accusers and their family members, that had tried to trap Daniel. It was an act of God, and the King witnessed the miracle and had his people honor Daniel's God. There are many instances of God coming to peoples aid during difficult trials. That's what's in the Bible. God wants us to know of His existence, His power, and His love."

"So why are you sharing these stories with me?"

"Because I want you to know that God is with us in our captivity, and He will come to our aid. Just as He will be there for you, if you accept Him. You don't have to live like this Zach." Chris was trying so hard to get through to Zach, he felt the urgency in completing his assignment.

"So, you think that Jesus is here, like your daughter said? Is he going to save you?"

"He saves us all, one way or another."

"It's too late for me. I don't think God wants someone like me in His mix, anyway." The shame was evident in his speech.

"God loves all His children. There is light in you, His light, and I believe He wants you to find it, so that you can walk away from the darkness that you have found yourself in. It's said in 2 Corinthians 6:17 (NASB), '*Therefore, COME OUT FROM THEIR MIDST AND BE SEPARATE,*' says the Lord. '*AND DO NOT TOUCH WHAT IS UNCLEAN; And I will welcome you.*' God wants to show you that there is a better way to live.

'*Walk with the wise and become wise, for a companion of fools suffers harm* (Proverbs 13:20 NIV).'"

"What harm do you suppose we are in?"

Zach was thinking about the trouble now, he knew what they were doing was wrong. It was apparent that they would get caught eventually. He was also very impressed with how much Chris knew of this Bible; he kept talking about. Wondering if there was more to it?

"I think you know that answer. It's for you to decide to separate yourself from it."

"How do you know so much?"

"About what?" Chris wasn't sure where his mind was going.

"You recite some book like you've memorized it or something."

"I've studied the Bible for a long time, and every time I read it, I learn something new. It's why it's called the Living Bible. Something is always being revealed in another way when you study His Word. I don't lean on my own understanding; I discern what God wants me to receive from Him at the time I am reading His Word."

"Are you saying the words on the pages speak to you?"

"Not out loud, but I feel them from within, as if they are speaking out loud. I'm being guided by the Holy Spirit. I walk in faith, which I believe demonstrates the light given to me. A light that is guiding me and giving me the ability to see light in you."

"Now you are off your rocker. I don't believe in spirits." Zach pushed back in his chair as if he was pushing away from Chris, thinking he was the one who had lost his mind.

"Well, it's supernatural for sure. Jesus sent the Holy Spirit to us as a helper and a guide, when He returned to heaven to sit on the throne, next to His Father."

"So, you think that this man called Jesus, is sitting in the clouds somewhere on a throne? Thought you said He was with us? You need to make up your mind." Confused by Chris's talking points.

"I believe it to be true, because I trust His Word. And I trust that you are following more than you are making out like you are."

He looked in Ellen's direction and he could see that she was plotting something, but he had no idea what was running through her head. He just knew that if he could get through to Zach it would give them some hope, that he would help them in some way. He was also convinced that it may help others, if they didn't make it out of this mess. He was planting a seed.

Ellen has always trusted in the Lord, no matter the events that came her way. She was feeling the prodding of God to do something to save her family. It was necessary for her to act on the opportunities that God presented her with. The lust in Jasper's eye was keenly felt and thought that it may be used to her advantage. But Chris is not going to like what she has in mind. The plot of Jael in the Bible came to mind.

Remembering what she had read in Judges 4, about Jael luring Sisera, a cruel commander of the Canaanites army who oppressed the Israelites for over twenty years, into her tent for false refuge. Having shown him kindness yet when given the right opportunity she didn't hesitate to act and drove a tent peg through his temple. Ignoring her fears and acting on God's prodding she played a role in the beginning of the end of the Canaanites reign. Ellen needed to play a part in the end of this captivity that they were in. She was confident in God's prodding.

The Scripture that came to mind was 2 Corinthians 3:4-6 (NASB). *"Such confidence we have through Christ toward God. Not that we are adequate in ourselves to consider anything as coming from ourselves, but our adequacy is from God, who also made us adequate as servants of a new covenant, not of the letter but of the Spirit; for the letter kills, but the Spirit gives life."*

Recognizing that they were battling for their lives, she knew who and what she was battling. *"Finally, be strong in the Lord and in the strength of His might. Put on the full armor of God, so that you will be able to stand firm against the schemes of the devil. For our struggle is not against flesh and blood, but against the rulers, against the powers, against the world forces of this darkness, against the spiritual forces of wickedness in the heavenly places* (Ephesians 6:10-12 NASB)."

When Ellen looked into Jasper's eyes, she only saw evil intent and lust, schemes of the devil. When the opportunity arose, she would lure him aside and God would show her the tools to take him down. She didn't have a tent peg, but God would put something in her path to use, even if it was the towel rod that Chris tried to use earlier. She wasn't sure how much she could endure, but if it gave Chris time to derail the other two it would be worth it.

Chris and Ellen both realized that their time was limited. At some point Louise would make a move to kidnap their daughter and give the order to kill them both. It was Chris' hope that he had gotten through to Zach, but it was apparent that he feared his family. Would he stand up against them to protect people he didn't know? There was a lot of uncertainty.

Chris was reflecting on what Elsie had said earlier. She stated that Jesus was in the room with them. Had she really seen Jesus? Was He still in the room? Would he step in at the right time to protect them from the heat, like he did with the three Hebrew men? This is what he says he believes; will he trust in Jesus? Like the three Hebrew men, he has faith that if he doesn't survive this trial, he takes comfort knowing where he is going. The verse that kept flashing in his head was, *"If our God Whom we serve is able to deliver us from the burning fiery furnace, he will deliver us out of your hand, O king* (Daniel 3:17 AMP)."

Ellen noticed Jasper staring in her direction again. It disgusted her, but the idea came to her that she must lure him out of the room. She started playing with her hair, then lowering her hands to her neck as if she was rubbing a sore neck, then arching her back, stretching in a provocative way just enough to capture his attention. Allowing her hands to fall to her waist, then to the top of her legs as she rubbed the top of them. It may have appeared as an innocent stretch from sitting so long to anyone else, but not to someone that was aroused by her every move.

Jasper watched intently and was practically foaming at the mouth. She had him where she wanted him, his gaze was locked on her for sure. Now to coerce him to the other room. With the signals she was giving him, he felt she was desiring him as well. Maybe there was something to the Stockholm syndrome he had heard about. Where hostages develop a bond with the captors, creating an emotional attachment. Whatever it was, he wanted a part of it.

Taking her husband out was an easy task, but his mother stood in the way. Although she was preoccupied with the little girl, maybe he could just show the woman to the bathroom, and they could both relieve themselves of the tension they were both experiencing. Jasper knew the outcome of disrespecting his mother, maybe she would excuse him, just this once.

45

Elsie wiggled in her chair, then started popping up and down a bit until Louise asked her what was wrong. Responding that she needed to potty. Apparently, all the juice she had been given had run its course through her little body. It was time to go, and she wanted her mommy to help her to the bathroom. As a modest little girl, she knew that she needed to undress to get on the big potty, it was a job for her mother. After a little bit of whining and looking a little panicked, Louise conceded that Ellen could help her in the bathroom, while she stood guard at the door.

Ellen was upset that her plan had been foiled by a potty break. She had Jasper right where she wanted him, and she didn't know if she'd have that same effect later. As she got up from her chair, she kept her eyes on Jasper and gave him a lingering look, like she'd be right back, and they could pick up where they left off. She could feel his eyes trailing after her, knowing he was hooked.

While in the bathroom maybe she'd see something she could use as a weapon. As she was assisting Elsie in undressing, it did occur to her that getting Louise separated from the other two might present another path to freedom. Now hoping that Chris was thinking the same thing. We have them separated, it's our opportunity to do something. It could all be very deadly, but the end game for them was likely a lethal end anyway.

Song "Heart of God" by Zach Williams

46

6

THE ENTRY

The police were closing in on the cabin. They did not come blazing up the mountainside with lights flashing and sirens blaring, they were wanting an element of surprise for fear that the Cassidy family would turn on the hostages, if they were still alive. They were holding out hope that they would find them alive and well, but the descriptions that had been depicted over the radio from previous crime scenes, didn't sound promising. It was likely a bloody crime event that they were to come across.

They came prepared with a medical emergency team that was instructed to remain a few miles away, until they were signaled to come closer. It was already known that bodies were present at the cabin above the one they were headed to, based on George's eyewitness account.

The team had discussed that this family didn't seem to be afraid of the law, nor did they show compassion for victims. Comments were made that the villains acted as if they had a death wish and the Sargent announced he was happy to oblige them. If it was necessary, shoot to kill, were the orders given. The Sargent didn't want any of his team going home in a body bag. It may be a long night for them all.

It was pitch dark and they were aware that any light could give them away, therefore night goggles were used to move forward up the hill to the cabin. Movements were slow and deliberate so as not to make more sound than necessary. It was good that George had described the layout of his cabin to them and where the points of entry were located.

George had not realized the importance of the details he had given them, how every bit of information was critical to a mission being successful. He had just wanted them to go blazing up the hill and rescue his family, but a well-planned approach saves lives.

The closer they got, the more they could see smoke coming from the cabin chimney. It was a good sign that they were still occupying the cabin.

They surrounded the cabin from the tree line, and then dispatched smaller teams to move onto the deck area. Windows were checked for movements within. No one was seen in George's room, so they tried the window to see if they could access the cabin. The window was shut tight, so a team member was left stationed at the window with his firearm pulled to take out any intruder if given an opportunity. It was assumed shooting through the glass at that point wouldn't matter as long as the assailant was taken out. They had been given the description of Chris and Ellen, so as not to get them confused with the others. Their job was to save the hostages and to remove the threat.

A team was posted at each entry to the cabin, waiting for the signal to move in. As soon as the team entered the cabin, the next flanking team was to follow suit, leaving one team at the tree line, in case someone managed to dart outside. They were calculating the opportune time to enter all at once to confuse the Cassidy's by creating quite the commotion. The sudden entry would throw them off and give them only seconds to take down the threat.

The Sargent saw Ellen and Elsie enter the bathroom, he was waiting to hear the location of Chris, and when that was confirmed, it was agreed having them separated was the perfect time to secure the site. The word was given to enter. God was definitely with them on the timing of things.

Chaos broke loose. The teams entered quickly and loudly to disorient everyone. As soon as the teams entered, the outside teams moved up to the deck area, to secure the surroundings, then entered for backup. Louise was easily subdued from the rear entry, she had just turned her back to the door at the time they accessed it and knocked her down, dislodging the shotgun from her hands. One officer handcuffed her while the other moved forward to the open room, while instructing Ellen to stay put. Ellen and Elsie hunkered down in the bathroom, jumping into the big tub again, in case bullets started to fly around.

The team at the front door startled Jasper and Zach completely. They were caught off guard, Jasper was daydreaming about Ellen coming back into the room, and Zach was preoccupied in conversation with Chris. Neither had not thought to post themselves outside guarding the cabin, they thought all threats were taken care of.

In most cases, they hit a place and were on the move down the road away from the crime scene. There had not been a need to secure their location before. They weren't exactly professionals, just desperate individuals.

Louise had been preoccupied with Elsie, trying to secure her confidence, thinking she would want to go freely with them, when she gave the order to move out. It had been her plan to leave at first light, taking Elsie with her to the car that belonged to the Chaplains. This would ensure Elsie 's comfort, being in her own vehicle, which would already have the car seat in it as well, which would save time. Confinement from the car seat would prove to be beneficial in this case, it wasn't a matter of safety, much less following the law to Louise. It would prevent Elsie from pushing back too much when she realized her parents weren't joining them.

If they couldn't find the car keys, they would just hotwire it, like they do most of the vehicles that they obtained. Moving from one vehicle to the next had become part of their routine in evading capture. A deceptive story would be contrived, detaining the parents, so that Jasper could deal with them permanently. If Jasper wanted to have his way with the woman, it didn't matter to her, as long as he didn't take his time. Once they decided to leave, they'd have to move fast.

The first officer through the door charged Jasper, knocking him down but he got up and scrambled to the bedroom, trying to take cover, not realizing there was another angle of threat upon him. The second officer had his revolver pointed at him ready to shoot, the minute Jasper walked through the bedroom door, the man posted outside the window shot him, taking him down permanently. It was a clean shot, right through the glass to his chest.

Zach could have turned and killed Chris, if he was a killer, or used him as a shield, but chose to face the music head on. He pulled his gun as soon as the action began, which did not end well for him. The second officer coming from the bedroom where Louise was caught, shot him in the back. As far as he was concerned it was a righteous kill. Zach had his gun pulled and everything was moving fast. The officer had to make a split-second decision to shoot so that Zach didn't fire on the other officers or turn on Chris.

Chris was devastated. He was talking with Zach one minute and chaos ensued the next, now he was watching this young man take his last breath. He was holding him in his arms praying over him. Not sure what to actually pray, because he was in such a state of confusion, but through his tears, he managed to call out to Jesus to save Zach.

The officer wasn't sure what he was witnessing. He had taken down the threat and this man was hovering over him like it was his son. Ellen came running to Chris's side with Elsie in toe. Grabbing Chris, seeing all the blood, checking him thoroughly, making sure he was not shot, then asking if he was alright. Turning and latching onto her upset and teary eyed, acknowledging that he was fine and glad she was safe. He looked down at Elsie, trying to smile, but he was too emotionally distraught.

Elsie grabbed Chris's legs, hugging her daddy, telling him it would be okay. Chris patted her back and thanked her, but he was crushed in spirit.

"Daddy, Zach is with Jesus." Elsie was trying to comfort her daddy.

"We hope that is true, my love." He said through teary eyes, his heart pounding from emotions that he was trying to control for the sake of his child. He knew she meant well.

"He is Daddy, I see him right there with Jesus." She was pointing off to the right.

All eyes in the room looked in the direction Elsie was pointing, but they saw nothing. One officer thought she had lost her mind, the other thought she was in shock and possibly seeing things from the trauma she had been under. Another officer was questioning if she had hit her head. The officers were calling the medics to come on up, wanting them to check the child out first.

Ellen and Chris smiled in the direction she was pointing and back at her. They were starting to realize the truth, they had a gifted child that was seeing something that they couldn't see.

Louise was wailing over the loss of her two boys. Cursing the officers and asking them what they had done. This seemed to be an odd thing coming from a woman who didn't mind taking other people's lives randomly. One might have felt sorry for her except for the fact that they knew how callous she really was. The ambulances were radioed, informing them of the status of the crime scene, and were told to come on in, the site had been secured. Lights were now turned on everywhere, inside and out. The police had brought lights to start processing the scene of the crime. Their next step was to check the other cabins in the area.

Song "God Really Loves Us" by Crowder

7

THE DAY TIME STOPPED

Everything seemed strangely peaceful. The chaos was so distant from where he was. As he looked around and patted himself down trying to figure things out. The first question asked was, "Where am I?"

Zach looked up at Jesus with a very confused look on his face, and then asked who He was. He didn't feel scared or even concerned, just a little confused. Without answering the first question directly, Jesus just smiled at him, and stated He was the Christ Jesus that Chris had been talking about.

"You mean, The Jesus? The one Chris said was my Savior?" He was already acknowledging Jesus as his savior without realizing it.

Jesus confirmed to Zach that He was the one spoken of in the Bible, specifically pointing out Philippians 2:9-11(NIV) as He recited it.

"*God exalted him to the highest place and gave him the name that is above every name, that at the name of Jesus every knee should bow, in heaven and on earth and under the earth, and every tongue acknowledge that Jesus Christ is Lord, to the glory of God the Father* (Philippians 2:9-11 NIV).'"

Jesus told him that He was his Savior if he received Him as such. Explaining that it's always a choice.

"Well, you just saved me from all of that." As he looked down at what appeared like a chaotic scene below him.

Jesus didn't save him from the scene that Zach was viewing. Jesus encouraged him to look closer and take in the fuller picture.

Zach looked down and realized his body was still on the scene, below him. "I'm dead?"

Jesus confirmed that he was for sure dead, at that moment.

"Where am I? And why are we here?" Zach was confused even more now that he realized he was dead.

Assuring Zach that he didn't need to worry about where he was, just the fact that he was there with Jesus, who wanted to give him an assignment.

"An assignment? What on earth are you talking about?"

If he was dead, how was he to have an assignment? It didn't make any sense. Of course, nothing was making any sense. It would have been assumed that he was dreaming except for the fact that he remembered being awake, talking to Chris just moments ago. The timing of things didn't seem possible.

Later Zach was even more surprised to find out that his assignment was not in heaven but on earth.

"Do you always talk in riddles? I'm a simple country boy and you just need to spell it out for me to understand."

It was time to clarify the scenario. Jesus shared with Zach, that He knew his heart and that he was not like the rest of his family. Explaining that Jasper was a hardened criminal, callous to the core, not open to receiving any kind of light. Which saddened His own heart. That his mother had a chance and lost it, she had become deceptive and cruel. Neither of them sought out something different to turn their lives around.

Further explaining that they were given opportunities to make different choices, they chose darkness and evil. However, Zach was different, he was approachable. Chris had seen the light in him, as well. That is why Chris had tried so hard to get through to him. Stating that no one is judged on what they do not know when the circumstances are not of their own making. Chris had given him an opportunity to know Jesus.

Now it was time for Zach to decide. Jesus asked the pertinent question, whether he was ready to accept Him as his Lord and Savior?

"You mean I can decide that right now?"

Still confused about his options and how all this was going to play out. And just what kind of assignment was he supposed to take on? It seemed strange to have the One who died for him, standing before him, asking if he would accept Him as the Son of God.

Jesus' tone was so endearing and loving, it captivated Zach. He just wanted to be hugged by Him as if he was a lost boy and was found. Jesus knew Zach's heart and knew that he hungered for something that would free him from the darkness that enveloped his life.

It had been laid on Chris's heart to try to get through to Zach to show him the mercy and kindness that his soul ached for. Jesus witnessed Zach's receptiveness of what Chris was telling him. He wanted to give Zach the opportunity to receive salvation. Jesus truly didn't want anyone to be lost. Jesus sees the potential in every man and desires for them to dedicate their life to Him, so that they can participate in His plans for each individual and for all of humanity.

Jesus spoke words from John 3:16 (NIV), wanting them to resonate with Zach.

"'For God so loved the world that he gave his one and only Son, that whoever believes in him shall not perish but have eternal life.'"

Looking at him wanting it to be revealed that He was that Son being spoken of in the passage, the same one that was standing before him, desiring for him to embrace eternal life. Once again, He spoke to Zach through Scripture.

"'I am the resurrection and the life; he who believes in Me will live even if he dies, and everyone who lives and believes in Me will never die, Do you believe this? (John 11:25,26 NASB).'"

Zach was stunned by the words Jesus was speaking. After all he was dead, but the one in front of him was now offering life. This was a difficult concept to comprehend as he looked down on his lifeless body below and back at Jesus, who he now longed to be with. There was a peace about Him that gave Zach comfort and stability, that he had never felt before.

At that point he knew that his existence could be different, where he was. Yet Jesus was offering him an assignment on earth. The tug that was compelling him was that he just wanted to stay in the comfort of Jesus's presence.

Jesus continued speaking to Zach. "'For the wages of sin is death, but the free gift of God is eternal life in Christ Jesus our Lord (Romans 6:23 NASB).'"

Sharing that those words were written about Him in the Bible, so that people can come to know who He is and what He has to offer.

It didn't make sense, but Zach was starting to understand a little more as they spent time together. Jesus continued to share with him words that were inspired by God written in Ecclesiastes 12:5-7 (NKJV).

"'Man goes to his everlasting home, And the mourners go about the streets or marketplaces. [Remember your Creator earnestly now] before the silver cord [of life] is snapped apart, or the golden bowl is broken, or the pitcher broken at the fountain, or the wheel broken at the cistern [and the whole circulatory system of the blood ceases to function]; and the dust returns to the ground it came from, and the spirit it returns to God who gave it.'"

"Am I dust now?"

Jesus reminded him that God created man from the dust of the earth and that the body returns to dust, but God also gave a spirit which came from Himself, the Father of Lights. Pointing out that a choice is given to return to Him, but one must believe in God's Son. Explaining that the One who laid down His life for him, just as it was done for all humanity, paid the price for everyone's sins. It was a decision to be made whether to accept the gift or not.

Pondering all that Jesus was saying, but he wasn't sure how to respond.

Jesus was reminding Zach that He was the doorway to home, and He was right there wanting to welcome him home.

"How can I not believe who you are, when you are standing in front of me, and I am seeing what is happening below me. Pardon my French, but that's a no brainer."

Jesus burst out laughing, you could say He had an instant love for this young man, but His love for him had always been present. He just wanted Zach to testify who He was and acknowledge Him as His Savior.

They continued to talk, and the questions bubbled up from Zach like a fountain. Jesus was enjoying the hunger he had for more knowledge about Himself and the message from the Bible that Chris had been sharing with him.

Zach thought back about Elsie's statement about seeing Jesus. And he asked the burning question, "Could she really see You?"

Jesus confirmed that she has a special gift as a seer, and yes, she had been able to witness Him watching over them. He further explained that

Elsie also has a special assignment on her life, one that she would embrace when she was older, she would be able to reveal heaven to the Body of Christ.

"What exactly does that mean?" Zach asked out of curiosity.

The details started to unfold that it meant she would have access to heaven, by way of visits, and she would be called to describe the trips to people, to awaken them as to what heaven is all about.

"So, when she said she went to heaven, she really did go to the actual heaven?"

Jesus smiled and reminded him where he was at that very moment.

"You mean I'm in heaven?"

Zach looked around trying to absorb all that he was seeing, wanting to capture everything in his memory. It would have been like a kid in a candy store trying to take in every kind of candy in every jar.

The biggest smile crossed Jesus' face as if it was an inside joke of some kind, while He shared that Zach would also have a story to tell when he was back on earth.

"So, I am not staying with you?" He didn't want to leave; this was still puzzling him.

No, was the simple answer given, before going into detail that Zach's assignment was on earth, if he was willing to accept it.

"What if I want to stay with you?"

Jesus understood how he felt being in a place of peace and total contentment, especially after living a life void of such comfort and acceptance. He knew how hard it would be to leave. But He was giving him an opportunity to do a great work for the Lord, which would affect many lives.

It was necessary to clarify for Zach, that He would always have a place prepared for him in heaven, when it was his time. It just wasn't his time to be there now. Jesus went on to state that He would prepare a mansion suited just for Zach one day. Pointing out that it is promised in the Bible in John 14:2,3 (NKJV).

"*In My Father's house are many mansions; if it were not so, I would have told you. I go to prepare a place for you. And if I go and prepare a place for you, I will come again and receive you to myself; that where I am, there you may be also.*'"

Time seemed to stand still. Much was being imparted to Zach, the more they were together the more Zach wanted to remain with Jesus. He had no idea how long he would have with Jesus, but he knew that there would be a limit to their intimate time. The scene below him seemed to remain frozen.

Jesus was in no hurry; He was in control of the situation. Zach was just absorbing all the information he could from Jesus while he had Him to himself. Jesus imparted a lot of knowledge to him in what seemed like a short time, but what is time when one controls eternity.

Zach had been given a gift at birth of evangelism from Father God, but had not developed it, because of his lack of knowledge and his life's circumstances. Jesus was giving him a second chance to use his gift. It was his assignment. Explaining to him that he wanted Zach to return to his body on earth and fulfill the destiny that God had laid out for him from the very beginning, for him to evangelize. Warning that the beginning of his journey might be a bit rocky.

Clarifying that he would have to serve some time in prison for taking part in the crimes that had been forged by his family. After all He was a God of justice and Zach would be held accountable for his part in the deaths of many innocent lives. Although there was judgment to be served out, Zach was assured that life would be different for him now. There would never be a time that he would be without Him, therefore that should embolden him.

Zach was further enlightened by Jesus, how God is gracious and just. When He quoted from the Prophet Isaiah. "*Therefore the LORD longs to be gracious to you, And therefore He waits on high to have compassion on you. For the LORD is a God of justice; How blessed are all those who long for Him* (Isaiah 30:18 NASB).'"

It was becoming clear to Zach; Jesus had always been longing for Zach to recognize who He was.

This made him feel special, made him feel loved and wanted.

There was a lot that Jesus was trying to teach Zach in the time they had together. Most importantly was for him to see how the Scriptures speak truth and that's what was to guide him in his future. By pointing out what was written in the Psalms as a start.

"'*The LORD abides forever; He has established His throne for judgment, And He will judge the world in righteousness; He will execute judgment for the peoples with equity. The LORD also will be a stronghold for the oppressed, A stronghold in times of trouble; And those who know Your name will put their trust in You, For You, O LORD, have not forsaken those who seek You* (Psalm 9:7-10 NASB).'"

"I don't know much but it sounds like I'm headed for trouble. I am definitely afraid of going to jail." Zach was simply speaking his truth.

Zach was called for the purpose of what Jesus was imparting to him at that very moment. A message for him to hold onto.

"'*Proclaim the name of the LORD: Ascribe greatness to our God. He is the Rock, His work is perfect; For all His ways are justice, A God of truth and without injustice; Righteous and upright is He* (Deuteronomy 32:4 NKJV).'"

Expressing to him, that verse alone should demonstrate that he had nothing to fear.

"I don't know about that. I can honestly say I don't know about a lot of things." Still concerned about where he was headed.

Smiling back at Zach realizing that he had no idea of his true potential, yet Jesus had seen it in him all along. It was now time to demonstrate the words that He wanted Zach to share with others that would strengthen not only him but for those that Zach would be encountering. Jesus wanted to assure him that he would not be on his own, but he had the capability to achieve great things.

"'*My Grace is sufficient for you, for My strength is made perfect in weakness* (2 Corinthians 12:9 NKJV).'"

Jesus laid his hands on Zach's shoulders as if shoring him up, giving him support. There was a need for him to fully understand Isaiah, the great prophet, and the message he delivered regarding comfort.

"'*He gives strength to the weary, And to him who lacks might He increases power. Though youths grow weary and tired, And vigorous young men stumble badly, Yet those who wait for the LORD Will gain new strength; They will mount up with wings like eagles, They will run and not get tired, They will walk and not become weary* (Isaiah 40:29-31 NASB).'"

Jesus pointed out to Zach that he was an eagle, one that takes flight, not a chicken who is limited to the ground. Zach needed to be awakened to his true identity in Christ.

"I like that, I'm an eagle." You could tell that he was visualizing himself soaring in the sky like an eagle.

More words of encouragement were given to Zach to share with others for where he would be going. It was a matter of renewing his mind, he was called to be different and heed the words spoken in Romans 12:2 (NIV84).

"*Do not conform any longer to the pattern of this world, but be transformed by the renewing of your mind. Then you will be able to test and approve what God's will is—his good, pleasing and perfect will.*"

"What does renewing of my mind mean? Are you giving me a new brain?" Asking with a puzzled look.

There was laughter over the image that Zach conjured up, before answering with an emphatic no, clearly stating that he had a perfectly good brain, he just hadn't been using all that was given to him. Then explaining that He was having him rethink the way he thought about things.

Going on to say, that every word presented to him in the Bible has deeper meaning than what is on the surface. That he would need to learn to search for the deeper intent of each Word. Knowing that what He was saying sounded difficult, but he wasn't going to be left on his own to figure it all out. Jesus brought up the fact the Holy Spirit was going to be with him to guide him and assist him as well. The Holy Spirit would lead him to a greater understanding.

Zach was strengthened by the words of encouragement. It was empowering to know that Jesus had such confidence in him. No one had ever shown him that kind of attention, or approval. Zach was spending quality time with the Lord of the Universe. That was still hard to wrap his head around. But he was absorbing all that was spoken and desiring more. God was giving him the ability to grasp and retain all that was being shared.

Jesus was assuring him that it was time to continue to bask in His presence, in order to stand against the devil's schemes, who put these men that he was to encounter, on the wrong path. It was His intent to give words of wisdom that would assist Zach with his assignment.

Explaining that it was just like Exodus 4:12 (NKJV), "*Now therefore, go, and I will be with your mouth and teach you what you shall say.*' Remember this as you come up against trouble, '*Do not say, I am a youth, For you shall go to all to whom I send you, And whatever I command you, you shall speak.*

Do not be afraid of their faces, For I am with you to deliver you (Jeremiah 1:7,8 NKJV).'"

Zach was like a sponge soaking up as much of the living water as he could. It was hard to believe that Jesus was putting so much faith in his ability to carry out this kind of assignment. But he was being placed to reach those that seemed untouchable.

Jesus quoted Isaiah 55:6-11 (NIV84), "'*Seek the LORD while he may be found; call on him while he is near. Let the wicked forsake his way and the evil man his thoughts. Let him turn to the LORD, and he will have mercy on him, and to our God, for he will pardon. 'For my thoughts are not your thoughts, neither are your ways my ways,' declares the LORD. As the heavens are higher than the earth, so are my ways higher than your ways and my thoughts than your thoughts.*

As the rain and the snow come down from heaven, and do not return to it without watering the earth and making it bud and flourish, so that it yields seed for the sower and bread for the eater, so is my word that goes out from my mouth: It will not return to me empty, but will accomplish what I desire and achieve the purpose for which I sent it.'"

His assignment was to evangelize to the prison inmates. Now having a powerful testimony to tell, which will pique the interest of many. Jesus shared stories of how His apostles were imprisoned yet their testimonies saved souls. Stressing the importance of getting through to these men, for they are lost souls, and Jesus was wanting them to have an opportunity to come home.

He was also making it known that it would make a difference to their lives in prison and to others when they were released into society. Their transformation would have a domino effect which could make a difference in so many ways. It was easy for Jesus to see the big picture; He was just hoping that Zach was starting to see it develop. Key points that were being stressed were the change of attitude, the change of thought, giving them hope where they now feel lost. It was a whole culture of people that he could affect while in prison.

Jesus wanted to encourage Zach to study the Bible daily and remember what He had spoken to him while they were together.

"'*For whatever was thus written in former days was written for our instruction, that by [our steadfast and patient] endurance and the encouragement [drawn] from the Scriptures we might hold fast to and cherish hope* (Romans 15:4 AMP). *This Book of the Law shall not depart from your mouth, but you shall meditate in it day and night, that you may observe to do according to all that is written in it. For then you will make your way prosperous, and then you will have good success. Have I not commanded you? Be strong and of good courage; do not be afraid, nor be dismayed, for the LORD your God is with you wherever you go* (Joshua 1:8,9 NKJV)."

Jesus continued to share with Zach more of what his mission would look like, by using Scripture, as He shared Matthew 16:19 (NKJV) with him.

"*And I will give you the keys of the kingdom of heaven, and whatever you bind on earth will be bound in heaven, and whatever you loose on earth will be loosed in heaven.*"

"What does that mean? Remember I told you I need things put to me plainly. No disrespect intended. But won't I need to explain it to others?"

Jesus smiled, enjoying his hunger for more understanding and willingness to ask questions. Sharing that He entrusted him with the ability to explain truths to the ones he would be engaging. Establishing trust and speaking truth was a crucial role in introducing The Gospel to the men he would encounter.

It was at that point that Jesus spoke about giving Zach the authority to bind and loose things on earth, confirming that heaven would make it happen according to His Will. It was as if a mantel was being transferred to Zach, when Jesus was entrusting him with some of His power. Jesus was directing him to study the Bible closely to know what aligns with His Word which carries power, so that in turn it would allow him to help others.

Then he asked Zach if what had been shared cleared things up for him?

Zach shook his head in affirmation, yet his words came out, "Clear as mud."

And they both laughed.

Jesus wasn't meaning to sugar coat anything for Zach, after all He is truth. It was revealed that he would run into opposition, possibly persecution, but he wasn't to fear.

"*It will turn out for you as an occasion for testimony. Therefore settle it in your hearts not to meditate beforehand on what you will answer; for I will give you a mouth and wisdom which all your adversaries will not be able to contradict or resist (Luke 21:13-15 NKJV).'"*

"So, I am to take on this challenge knowing that I am going to have a hard time and opposition? Nothing like charging a bull and expecting a good outcome."

Jesus once again had to remind Zach that he was given a helper, the Holy Spirit, that would guide him. Jesus wanted it made known that to these men that He loves them, and that having faith in Him was their access to heaven. Giving Zach an example, when He brought up that Chris had helped him find the door, now it was his turn to help others.

John 10:9,10 (NKJV) was referenced by Jesus. "*'I am the door. If anyone enters by Me, he will be saved, and will go in and out and find pasture. The thief does not come except to steal, and to kill, and to destroy. I have come that they may have life, and that they may have it more abundantly.'*"

Zach was understanding more and more of Jesus' message but what he wanted to know now was how long he would be in prison? Wanting to know what to expect, as well as what life would look like afterwards for him?

Jesus assured him that his assignment would take a while, but he is young and would make the most of his mission while in prison. He would not ever be alone; Jesus would always be with him, which was something that had been repeatedly told him, so that it would sink into his soul.

Jesus leaned into Zach, asking that he listen carefully to the words He wanted to share with him, stating the importance of him embracing them.

"*'The Lord is my Strength and my [impenetrable] Shield; my heart trusts in, relies on, and confidently leans on Him, and I am helped; therefore my heart greatly rejoices, and with my song will I praise Him. The Lord is their [unyielding] Strength, and He is the Stronghold of salvation to [me] His anointed. Save your people and bless Your heritage; nourish and shepherd them and carry them forever (Psalm 28:7-9 AMP).'*"

Jesus went on to reveal that Zach would have to testify against his mother, which He understood would be difficult, yet necessary. However, this would also end up helping in his own sentencing. Warning that her deceptive ways could influence some jurors, it was his testimony that would ensure her incarceration which was considered what was best for her right now. She needed restraint and order in her life. Life's circumstances had hardened her heart, and she was a danger to society. Leaving him with the hope that there would be an opportunity for her to repent once again, but as always, it was her choice.

Zach wasn't sure that it was love that he felt for his mother, possibly concern. He had been raised to respect her out of fear. Thoughts of the possibility of him evangelizing to her came to mind and Jesus smiled, for He knew his heart.

They walked and talked together which seemed like a lifetime and yet also seemed like no time at all. Time doesn't exist in heaven. But the moment did come that Jesus was to send Zach back to his body. There is no fear in heaven, so that wasn't felt by Zach, but he did long to stay with Jesus. Peace came over him knowing that Jesus' words were true, he would never be alone and that he would come back home when his assignment was complete.

Jesus also shared John 16:33 (NKJV) with him. "*These things I have spoken to you, that in Me you may have peace. In the World you will have tribulation; but be of good cheer, I have overcome the world.*"

Taking Zach's shoulders and drawing him in close to get his full attention once again, He spoke words from (Isaiah 41:10-13 NASB).

"*Do not fear, for I am with you; Do not anxiously look about you, for I am your God. I will strengthen you, surely I will help you, Surely I will uphold you with My righteous right hand. Behold, all those who are angered at you will be shamed and dishonored; Those who contend with you will be as nothing and will perish. You will seek those who quarrel with you, but will not find them, Those who war with you will be as nothing and nonexistent. For I am the LORD your God, who upholds your right hand, Who says to you, 'Do not fear, I will help you.'*"

Zach grasped hold of Jesus and gave Him a hug knowing that his time with Him was short and coming to a close. Jesus felt the love from Zach, but He also knew his future and was so proud of the work that he was to accomplish.

Jesus continued to speak to him with His written Word as a way for him to remember it, and to reflect on it.

"*My son, if you accept my words and store up my commands within you, turning your ear to wisdom and applying your heart to understanding, and if you call out for insight and cry aloud for understanding, and if you look for it as for silver and search for it as for hidden treasure, then you will understand the fear of the LORD and find the knowledge of God* (Proverbs 2:1-5 NIV84).'"

It pleased Jesus to use His own written Word, knowing that it would be a good reference for Zach when he read it in the Bible and saw the actual words written down, it would be like a special memory, so that he could grasp this moment with Jesus and again hear His voice.

It had become time for Zach to start his new path. The last words Jesus spoke before returning him to his body would stay with him forever.

"'*Seek the LORD and His strength; Seek His face evermore! Remember His marvelous works which He has done, His wonders, and the judgments of His mouth.* (Psalm 105:4,5 NKJV).'"

Song "Love Me Like I Am" by For King & Country, Jordin Sparks

PRAYERS ANSWERED

The room was filled with officers collecting evidence. They appeared to ignore Chris and Ellen's attempt to save a life. Chris and Ellen were both praying over Zach's body with tears in their eyes. Although Ellen may not have felt the same way as Chris, she saw how hard he had witnessed to this young man, and she loved her husband, so she joined in his sorrow. They cried for a lost soul that Chris saw light in.

Chris was still administering CPR and Ellen was laying hands on his head and declaring healing in Jesus' name. Aware that Chris had tried to save Zach's soul, yet they didn't have enough time to get him to confess and accept Jesus as his Savior, they were standing in the gap for him through prayer. Although Elsie had stated that she saw Zach with Jesus, so there was a chance that Jesus accepted him based on his heart not his words.

Ellen was quoting Scripture regarding the authority that Jesus left for us to live by. Too many people overlook the power and gift that was left to humanity. Not Ellen she for one believes and uses God's Words to see His power performed. Starting with Psalm 19:14 (NASB) continuing to read through Scripture that she felt would make a difference.

"*Let the words of my mouth and the meditation of my heart Be acceptable in Your sight, O LORD, my rock and my Redeemer.'*

'*May the LORD answer you in the day of trouble! May the name of the God of Jacob set you securely on high! May He send you help from the sanctuary and support you from Zion! (Psalm 20:1,2 NASB).'*

'Now God has not only raised the Lord, but will also raise us up through His power (1 Corinthians 6:14 NASB).'

'And He gave them power and authority over all the demons and to heal diseases. And He sent them out to proclaim the kingdom of God and to perform healing (Luke 9:1,2 NASB).'

'The kingdom of heaven is at hand. Heal the sick, raise the dead, cleanse the lepers, cast out demons. Freely you received, freely give (Matthew 10:7,8 NASB).'"

Chris slowly stopped the compressions and spoke boldly over Zach's lifeless body.

"God, you hear our cries. You have witnessed the heart of this man. Let his healing take place, may he rise up and overcome this wound. You have said in Your Word, *'While You extend Your hand to heal, and signs and wonders take place through the name of Your holy servant Jesus* (Acts 4:30 NASB).' We are calling on you Jesus, act now before it is too late."

Chris's heart quaked at the thought that he had been too late. But he hung on to the thought that his daughter said Jesus was present in the room with them, so he continued praying boldly in hopes that Jesus was hearing their prayers. Even though the paramedics were there and trying to remove the body, he was pushing them aside and clinging to Zach pronouncing more Scripture over him.

"*'Entrusting Himself to Him who judges righteously; and He Himself bore our sins in His body on the cross, so that we might die to sin and live to righteousness; for by His wounds you were healed. For you were continually straying like sheep, but now you have returned to the Shepherd and Guardian of your souls* (1 Peter 2:23-25 NASB).'"

Suddenly there was a heartbeat detected. It scared the paramedic, and he jumped back startled and fearful. He didn't know what to make of the situation, it was clear that the body he saw had lost too much blood and had been dead too long to recover.

Elsie could see Jesus standing over Zach and announced His presence in the room. Excited to see Jesus again yet confused by everyone else's surprised actions. The others in the room looked around as if they were looking for a ghost which made Elsie laugh.

Giggling, she asked her mom why everyone was acting so funny. Ellen smiled through the tears of joy and hugged Elsie with a clinging hug, not knowing really what to say about what had just happened. But what came to her mind was when Jesus raised the widow's son from the dead. They must have reacted in a similar way.

Recalling the story that is found in Luke, and smiled, thinking God is so good.

"*When the Lord saw her, He had compassion on her and said to her, 'Do not weep.' Then He came and touched the open coffin, and those who carried him stood still. And He said, 'Young man, I say to you, arise.' So he who was dead sat up and began to speak. And He presented him to his mother* (Luke 7:13-15 NKJV)."

Zach sat up a bit dazed, but alive. There was blood all around him, his blood, but there was no wound. Eye contact was made with Chris, and he smiled big while proceeding to thank him for believing in him and introducing him to Jesus.

Chris was so overjoyed he didn't know what to say, he was simply speechless as he hugged Zach and praised God for giving him a second chance at life. They had all witnessed a miracle.

Everyone in the room was overwhelmed by what they witnessed; it took a few minutes to process that they weren't dreaming what had just taken place. As soon as the paramedics finished examining Zach, they backed away still stunned, unable to explain what had happened.

The officer wasn't sure how to respond, except to continue his job, so he stepped forward to read him his rights and to handcuff him. Zach thanked the officer and stated that he wouldn't be any trouble. It was a most unusual statement under the circumstances, but nothing seemed normal at that moment.

Chris was assuring Zach that everything would be alright. Zach was shaking his head as if he knew everything was going to be alright and for Chris not to worry. Chris continued with words of encouragement, stating that he would come and check on him, as soon as he was allowed. Realizing there were a lot of questions he wanted to ask him. Something miraculous had just taken place and he knew there was more to the story.

Then he directed his questions to the officer. Asking him where Zach would be taken, and would they be allowed to see him after he was processed? The specifics were shared, and they were preparing to take

Zach away, when he turned and spoke to Chris as if it was something he needed to hear.

"Heaven is real, and your daughter has been there." He looked in Elsie's direction and smiled, directing his remark to her now. "I think you know you have a special assignment from God."

Elsie smiled back at him conveying that she knew what he was talking about. She was happy that he understood. Although she didn't completely understand her assignment yet.

Zach then turned to Chris again and said, "*I can do all things through Him who strengthens me* (Philippians 4:13 NASB).'" Then he followed it up with, "*Behold, God is my salvation, I will trust and not be afraid; For the LORD GOD is my strength and song, And He has become my salvation* (Isaiah 12:2 NASB).'"

Chris was beaming with a smile that could light up any room, the only tears rolling down his face were tears of joy. Only God could transform someone like that in such a short span of time. Yet he knew that it was God that had given him the right words to say to Zach, assisting him in quoting Scripture that needed to be told.

Just as now when he spoke. "*But God, being rich in mercy, because of His great love with which He loved us, even when we were dead in our transgressions, made us alive together with Christ (by grace you have been saved), and raised us up with Him, and seated us with Him in the heavenly places in Christ Jesus, so that in the ages to come He might show the surpassing riches of His grace in kindness toward us in Christ Jesus. For by grace you have been saved through faith; and that not of yourselves, it is the gift of God* (Ephesians 2:4-8 NASB).'"

The paramedics were wheeling Zach out on a gurney, although he could walk out on his own. They were still trying to comprehend someone being shot, pronounced dead, then was breathing with apparently no side effects, not even a wound. It was best to keep an eye on him.

Thinking spontaneously, Ellen ran to Zach's side and placed a Bible in his hands, lovingly patted his hands over the Bible and told him to keep it close. She looked up at the paramedics and the officer and asked that he be able to keep it at his side. Based on what they just witnessed they were not about to remove a Bible from him. Then she turned to look into Zach's eyes and recited a verse from Ephesians 6:10 (AMP).

"'*Be strong in the Lord [be empowered through your union with Him]; draw your strength from Him [that strength which His boundless might provides].*'"

Chris, Ellen, and Elsie were wrapped in each other's arms, praising God for answering their prayers and allowing them to witness a miracle. Then Chris looked down at Elsie and apologized for ever doubting her. They were all thankful to be alive. Then it occurred to them, how did the police know where they were? Instead of answering a bunch of questions the police had, they started asking their own questions.

"Had someone reported gunfire?" Chris asked digging for more information.

"A witness called in a report of gunfire and hostages." One officer replied.

"Are their survivors?" Ellen was relieved to know that someone had made it out of this mess.

"Apparently so." The officer really didn't know all the details as to where the information had come from.

"Praise the Lord, that lives were saved." Came from both Chris and Ellen.

"Yes, I heard that this crew had been on quite the rampage, all the way from Tennessee."

All the facts were still unclear about who the Cassidy's were and what they had gotten away with, until now. Chris had hoped that the other cabins had been empty, and no one else had been shot but the ones he witnessed, and of course, Pop. He was telling the officer what he had seen earlier in the day and where he thought the bodies were located. The officer was assuring him that a team was already on that. They came prepared and had gotten a report from the witness that called in for help.

Another officer walked into the cabin at that time, he was one of the local policemen who had come from Miss Mae's house. Overhearing the conversation, he realized that the Chaplains were unaware that Pop, George Johnson, was alive. He had endeared himself to all the officers that had come by Miss Mae's house.

They were all amazed at his bravery and endurance through his ordeal, at his age. Of course, he had given witness to them, that God had been with him through it all. This young officer was pleased to give them the update on Pop. They were all floored and overjoyed, wanting to know every little detail. It was as if they had experienced another resurrection. The next critical question was, could they see him?

Song "In Jesus Name (God of Possible)" by Katy Nichole

9

REUNITED

The officer was assisting them with their things and wanting to drive them to where George Johnson was located to reunite the family. The officer was sharing how impressed he was with her father's maneuvers to find safety and refuge at Miss Mae's. Being a quick thinker and keeping a level head about him, saved his life and theirs. Ellen was pleased to hear how brave her father had been, most importantly she was relieved to know that he was alive.

It was common practice that after such an ordeal, an officer was to escort the victims to a safe and secure sight. With emotions so high after such an event the police didn't think that it was a good idea for them to drive, plus it was felt that the family needed a secure escort. Truth was, they could have floated down the mountain, they were on such a cloud nine moment, from their experience, but they accepted the offer due to the hour and realizing the obvious, they didn't know where they were going.

George had stayed at Miss Mae's, which was considered a good point of contact with an officer posted for their protection. No one was sure exactly what was going to ensue after they confronted the Cassidy's at the cabin.

The officer and family made their way down the mountain a little way to Miss Mae's house, with the lights flashing, yet no sirens, so as to avoid disturbing others at such a late hour. Upon pulling up to the little farmhouse, Pop ran out the door to greet them with a big hug.

Miss Mae followed him out to the porch and witnessed their joyful reunion. After thinking that he was dead, this was another resurrection moment for Ellen and Chris for sure. Ellen hugged him and had to hold his face in her hands to make sure he was really there, in front of her. Pop was so thankful that they were alive and well; tears streamed from his face. He too was grabbing hold and not wanting to let go of them, staring into their eyes with joy and relief and praising God for His goodness and ability to answer prayers.

The Scripture that came to mind was from Genesis 48:11 (NASB), *"I never expected to see your face, and behold, God has let me see your children as well."*

Miss Mae gave them a minute to reunite and then she started encouraging them to come on inside where it was warm. She was ready to dote on them and show them some of her hospitality. When they came into the light, she noticed blood on all three of them. A horrified look crossed her face, and a gasp was released, then questions proceeded to unfold.

"Are you all alright? Does anyone need medical attention?" She was rushing towards the first towel she could grab.

Pop looked down at his children in the light and was shocked by the amount of blood that covered their clothing. He grabbed Ellen and was searching her body for a wound. Ellen assured him they were all fine. That it was not their blood. Apologizing for the fright, then suggested that they should change their clothes, if it was alright with Miss Mae. Who of course insisted that she wash their things promptly as soon as they got out of them.

Then Miss Mae busied herself with getting everyone something to eat and drink, including the officers. Who happened to love their detail at Miss Mae's for that very reason, there was always something good coming out of her kitchen. This was a very exciting evening for her, and she was happy to serve the family in any way she could, as well as the police that had been so helpful.

Curiosity was getting the best of her, but she knew that it would be too much for the family to relive it all at that very moment, so she didn't dig for information, she remained silent regarding the events of the day. Her job at the moment was to make them all comfortable. They would share what they could when they were ready.

There was discussion from the officer about getting them a hotel room in town. Miss Mae interjected quickly and said that her home was open to them for as long as they needed it. She enjoyed the company and being of service to them. Her hospitality was greatly appreciated, but the officer was stating that it would be more than just a night's stay. Interviews would take place in the morning, and he wasn't sure how long they would want them to stick around town to process things.

The invitation still stood, and she was being persistent about them staying with her, there was plenty of room. One look at Elsie, and it was clear she was getting tired; after getting something to eat, her little body was ready to unwind. Miss Mae insisted that she crawl into her bed and get some sleep. Walking down the hall, hands flailing, assigning rooms to the others, not taking no for an answer. In her mind it was a done deal.

The officers were assigned to their vehicles to stay close to the radio and would take the family into town in the morning, based on orders given by the captain. Pop looked back at Miss Mae and asked her where she was going to sleep, now that she had given up her own bed. Miss Mae smiled and looked over at her big recliner.

"I spend a lot of my evenings in that big chair, no need for tonight to be any different."

"Are you sure you will be comfortable there?" Pop was not wanting to roust her out of her own beds, she had already done so much for them.

"I'm as sure as I know the sun is coming up in a few hours. Now get on to bed and get some rest so that you can think clearly in the morning."

Everyone shuffled off to bed, the officers secured the home and settled in their car.

Miss Mae pulled a blanket over herself and nestled right comfortably in her chair for a cat nap, before she was up and preparing breakfast for everyone. The house was filled with the aroma of fresh bread and bacon frying. She was beating the eggs and preparing to place them in the pan when Pop entered the kitchen, asking if he could help with anything.

"Pull some juice and milk from the refrigerator. I'm not sure which Elsie prefers, but I believe she will be the first one to come scampering in here wanting something to eat."

"You are right about that."

Although the officers were the first to appear at the back door. They didn't want to miss out on Miss Mae's breakfast feast. It was one of the perks for pulling an all-nighter in the car. While pouring the officers some coffee, Elsie came running into the room gleefully wanting to know if she could have some bacon. Having smelled it throughout the house it had her mouth watering. First things first, she gave Pop a big hug and then she hugged Miss Mae around the waist, as if she had known her forever, then thanked her for letting her sleep in her big bed.

Elsie then asked, "Did you know that you have a big cat that likes to sleep in your bed?"

"Yes, that is Pearl. I think she sleeps there more than I do, so you might want to thank her for sharing her bed with you." Miss Mae loved the attention and loved giving special attention to Elsie.

"I did that this morning. I also thanked her for keeping me warm. She practically slept on top of me." Elsie stated with a big smile on her face, loving the experience of having a pet around.

"She must really like you. She normally avoids people she doesn't know."

"I'm not people, I'm Elsie." She stated in a matter-of-fact way.

"Of course, you are."

Once Ellen and Chris entered the room, Pop insisted on giving thanks to the Lord for His care and provision. He also thanked Miss Mae for her hospitality and the wonderful feast she prepared for them to celebrate their ability to be reunited. They joined hands and Pop proceeded to recite Scripture for the rest of his blessing.

"*BEHOLD, how good and how pleasant it is For brethren to dwell together in unity! (Psalm 133:1 NKJV).*" Hands squeezed one another.

And he followed up with, "*One generation shall praise Your works to another, And shall declare Your mighty acts. I will meditate on the glorious splendor of Your majesty, And on Your wondrous works. Men shall speak of the might of Your awesome acts, And I will declare Your greatness. They shall utter the memory of Your great goodness, And shall sing of Your righteousness. The LORD is near to all who call upon Him, To all who call upon Him in truth. He will fulfill the desire of those who fear Him; He also will hear their cry and save them. The LORD preserves all who love Him, But all the wicked He will destroy. My mouth shall speak the praise of the LORD, And all flesh shall bless His holy name Forever and ever (Psalm 145:4-7, 18-21 NKJV).*"

It was one of those moments that you just wanted to continue to praise God so Chris added, *"'Believe on the Lord Jesus Christ, and you will be saved, you and your household* (Acts 16:31 NKJV).'"

As they remained with their heads bowed to take in the full blessing of what God had provided them, Chris continued with, *"'So you shall rejoice in every good thing which the LORD your God has given to you and your house, you and the Levite and the stranger who is among you* (Deuteronomy 26:11 NKJV).'"

Chris looked around the room at Miss Mae and the officers and thanked them for being there when his family needed them. He prayed that God would bless them fully for the part that they played in rescuing his family and the hospitality that had been shown them. He then looked at his wife and thanked her for being a strong spiritual woman, who had demonstrated strength through an immense time in their lives.

Then he recited 1 Corinthians 7:14 (NLT). *"'For the believing wife brings holiness to her marriage, and the believing husband brings holiness to his marriage. Otherwise, your children would not be holy, but now they are holy.'"*

Chris put his arms around Elsie and hugged her and praised the Lord for such a gift as this special child.

Elsie was pleased that her father was doting on her, but she was eager to dig into the feast provided by Miss Mae before everything got cold.

"Let's eat!"

Pop was unaware of what was being referred to in Chris's comments, but Ellen and Chris knew, and soon Pop would fully understand what Chris was talking about. Chris wanted it to be just family in the revealing of the explanation. Elsie was beaming with warm smiles and enjoying her bacon while soaking in the love and attention she was receiving. She really didn't fully understand what was going on, but she loved seeing her family together again and everyone seemed so happy.

All her experiences with Jesus were normal to her. The ability to see Jesus and participate in her visits to heaven, were not clearly understood as a unique gift from God, that others didn't share in. As she matured Jesus would reveal more and more to her to share with others and she would have a fuller understanding of what her assignment was about.

Miss Mae was capturing the beauty and warmth of the moment. She loved having a full house. It was her hope that she had made new friends and that they would come by to see her from time to time. Bribing the officers to come by was one thing, but to have a family come by and visit would seem more like she was a part of something bigger.

Conversations continued around the breakfast table about where they were to stay and how long they would have to be held up in town. It had been explained that they couldn't go back to the cabin, because it was a crime scene. At this point they even shuddered at the thought of returning to the cabin. A place where they were held captive, their child was almost kidnapped, they were almost killed, and they witnessed death.

Miss Mae insisted that they stay with her and prolong their visit. Insisting that she had plenty of room to share and she would cook for them, so they wouldn't have to worry about meals. She was selling the idea and went so far as to say that Elsie would have plenty of room to run and play outside, they wouldn't have that in a hotel room.

The officers shrugged their shoulders as if it was up to the family, they just wanted them to show up for the questioning and the prehearing. It wasn't clear how long the officers would be posted with the family, that may end after today. They mentioned that they would see that their car was brought to them so that they could avoid returning to the cabin.

This first one on board was Elsie, who wanted to stay with Pearl and assist Miss Mae in the kitchen. Announcing that Pearl would miss her. Her parents really didn't want to traumatize her anymore, so the prospect of staying became more appealing as they laid out the pros and cons. It also seemed to resolve the issue of what to do with Elsie, while they were being questioned again. They accepted Miss Mae's offer, and she started planning the next meal, as she went to fetch their cleaned clothes from the night before. Elsie was off to find Pearl and tell her the good news.

Chris was anxious to see Zach and was asking the officers if that would be possible today. The officer was unsure of that procedure but would follow up on it for him. He wanted Zach to know that he was going to support him through this whole ordeal, he was not going to go through this alone. There was also the burning question as to what Zach experienced with Jesus.

Song "Who You Say I Am" by Hillsong Worship

10

THE COURTROOM

The arraignment before the judge took place quickly. The evidence was stacked against them, and it seemed hopeless for Zach. Jasper didn't survive to face the music, which was likely his plan all along. Louise would have preferred being shot and killed over being locked up in a cell. Zach had a different perspective of what was to happen, his attitude was one of almost gratitude for being arrested. He knew his assignment was behind those bars and he embraced what Jesus had asked him to do with enthusiasm. He wasn't afraid, because he knew who was with him and that nothing was impossible with Jesus on his side.

After all, he had died and been to heaven and survived. If he died again, he knew where he would be going, and it was a matter of looking forward to being with Jesus once more in a place of calm, peace and contentment. It was a mindset of freedom, although his life would be behind bars for an unknown time. His mood and demeanor baffled the guards and even the judge. At one point the judge even stated that it looked like he was excited about going to prison.

Zach's remark was, "The sooner I get there the sooner I can start my assignment for God."

The judge ordered a psychiatric evaluation to do be conducted on Zach. There was plenty of time for that. The case wouldn't move forward until the crime scenes at The Cabins were fully developed and a case established against each of them, so there was time for him to be evaluated.

The judge wanted to know how to speak to him, as an insane man or an enlightened one.

The attorney assigned to Zach was already advising him to take the stand against his mother. Zach assured him he was ready for that, and he knew that was coming. He believed it was for her own good. Again, his responses were confusing those in charge of his case.

Based on some of the reports coming in, survivors from other crime scenes were giving statements that were surprisingly helpful in Zach's court case. After the shock of the events, they had realized that Zach wasn't the one killing people, he had allowed individuals to escape death. It was revealed that he wasn't the hardened criminal that they thought they were to fear, yet he was traveling with psychopaths.

When Zach heard the reports that were given, he was grateful. Thoughts of how good God truly is, flooded his mind, and he was ready to share that knowledge with others.

Talk travels fast behind bars. It had passed around the prison that a kid was coming in that had been part of a deadly gang. Some feared him and some wanted to challenge him. The guard that had been with him at the small jail cell warned Zach that there would be trouble when he got transferred to the county jail.

Zach had already started his witnessing behind bars with the guard, who listened intently to what he had to say. His story was quite compelling. Zach even amazed himself, he had always been the quiet one, a man of few words, and now he couldn't stop himself from talking about his experiences. He believed Jesus had given him a special boldness, where the right words flowed out at the right time.

It was as if the Word was spoken from the Lord, just as it was written in Deuteronomy 18:18,19 (NASB). *"I will raise up a prophet from among their countrymen like you, and I will put My words in his mouth, and he shall speak to them all that I command him. It will come about that whoever will not listen to My words which he shall speak in My name, I Myself will require it of him."*

He remembered that Jesus told him not to rely on his own strength but put his trust in the Lord and He would assist him.

As he was studying the Bible, he read in Jeremiah 17:7 (NIV), *"Blessed is the one who trusts in the LORD, whose confidence is in him."* This encouraged him that much more, as well as the Word in Acts 4:29,30 (NIV), *"Lord, consider their threats and enable your servants to speak your word with great boldness. Stretch out your hand to heal and perform signs and wonders through the name of your holy servant Jesus."*

Miracles were something he could speak to them about because he was a walking miracle. Being shot, having bled out, and yet he walked away unscathed as if nothing happened.

The Bible Chris and Ellen had given him was always with him, he clung to it as if he were holding onto Jesus. If there was any fear in him, it was not evident. He was confident that Jesus was with him, and his assignment was all that he cared about. Zach was even amazed at how easy it was to read the Word and retain it so quickly. It was as if he had been given a special gift of memorization. Possibly the fact that he had been with Jesus made it all seem clearer to him and easier to retain.

The day rolled around when Chris was finally able to visit him, and they hugged each other as if they were long lost brothers. No one would have suspected that Zach had been the one to hold Chris and his family hostage. Chris recognized that they were brothers in Christ, and he had come there for spiritual support, not realizing that Zach would be the one to strengthen his faith.

First, he wanted to know how he was being treated, then if he needed anything, before he came to the heart of the matter. What happened that night? Zach just reached out and hugged Chris again and then thanked him with his whole heart.

"Thank you for introducing me to life, through Jesus." He smiled big.

"So, you saw Jesus?" Chris was so curious about the actual events of that evening he could hardly contain himself.

"Oh yes, He was with me in Heaven. It's quite the place." He didn't elaborate on the place as much as he went on about being with Jesus who showed him so much love. His focus was Jesus.

"Jesus allowed me to choose life with Him and He taught me a lot about the Bible. Answers to all things in life are found in the Bible, but I think you already know that, Chris." Zach stated confidently.

"You talk as if you were there a long time?" Chris seemed surprised.

"There was a lot said in the time I was with Him. I think time stopped, because I could see my body and all of you below me, and everything was frozen." He was trying to explain it the way he saw it.

"He is the Lord of all things, including time. So, I guess that makes sense." Chris figured it was something you have to experience to fully understand it.

There was so much to share with Chris, but the guard insisted that their time was up. How could this be, Chris felt as if he had just walked through the door. Chris was frustrated at the time limit, there was so much to ask and so much for Zach to tell him about. It was even thought that it would be nice if Jesus could freeze a little time for them to finish their visit.

Although Zach was able to share that he had been given an assignment to conduct in prison, and that he was excited about how God was going to work behind the bars to help these men enter society as productive men. Chris loved that Zach was giving God the credit for the work that would take place. Encouragement was given to him before he left, and he stated that he would help him in any way that was needed. If he needed additional Bibles, he'd see that he got them to the prison that he was being taken to. Once again, the guard was nudging and calling time.

Zach smiled and stated, "The guard might be the first to need one of those Bibles."

Getting up from the table, moving toward the door, Zach turned and mentioned Elsie again. He quickly shared what Jesus had told him about Elsie's assignment on her life. How she was going to make trips back and forth to heaven and reveal heaven to people. God wants people to desire a relationship with Him and He feels if He lets them know what heaven is about, they won't fear Him or death. Zach's spirit just beamed with joy because he had seen some of what she would be sharing.

Chris was holding back tears of joy seeing how Zach had changed. Realizing he was allowed to let his light shine, it was very bright. The verse that came to mind was Isaiah 60:1,2 (NKJV), *"Arise, shine; For your light has come! And the glory of the LORD is risen upon you. For behold, the darkness shall cover the earth, And deep darkness the people; But the LORD will arise over you, And His glory will be seen upon you."*

Chris promised to be with Zach during the court hearings and felt sure Ellen would be there as often as she could.

Zach responded. "All is well."

He smiled back at Chris and made sure the guard was listening as he quoted Ephesians 1:11-23 (NASB). "'*We have obtained an inheritance, having been predestined according to His purpose who works all things after the counsel of His will, to the end that we who were the first to hope in Christ would be to the praise of His glory. In Him, you also, after listening to the message of truth, the gospel of your salvation—have also believed, you were sealed in Him with the Holy Spirit of promise, who is given as a pledge of our inheritance, with a view to the redemption of God's own possession, to the praise of His glory.*

For this reason, I too, having heard of the faith in the Lord Jesus which exists among you and your love for all the saints, do not cease giving thanks for you, while making mention of you in my prayers; that the God of our Lord Jesus Christ, the Father of glory, may give to you a spirit of wisdom and of revelation in the knowledge of Him. I pray that the eyes of your heart may be enlightened, so that you will know what is the hope of His calling, what are the riches of the glory of His inheritance in the saints, and what is the surpassing greatness of His power toward us who believe.

These are in accordance with the working of the strength of His might which He brought about in Christ, when He raised Him from the dead and seated Him at His right hand in the heavenly places, far above all rule and authority and power and dominion, and every name that is named, not only in this age but also in the one to come. And He put all things in subjection under His feet, and gave Him as head over all things to the church, which is His body, the fullness of Him who fills all in all.'"

Chris was utterly amazed at his transformation, how on earth was he able to quote Scripture like that not having studied the Bible? He couldn't wait to share what he just witnessed with Ellen.

"You just quoted Scripture word for word." He wanted the guard to also witness the amazing feat.

"Yes, ain't it grand what God can do. He has worked all this out according to His will and I get to be a part of it. I'm so excited to see what else He has in store. I believe that Word was for you, Chris. You were sealed with a promise, it's your love of humanity that God admires. He knows your works. You didn't give up on me and I know you won't give up on

others. He has blessed you with a child that will reveal things to the world about Him. Watch over her."

Chris nodded as if he had every intention of doing just that.

"He has a calling on your life that you need to seek out. I've had that opportunity to be raised up from the dead into heavenly places, not many get that opportunity, and it's amazing the joy that one feels when you are in the presence of the Lord. I don't fear anything that man can throw at me. I appreciate your prayers because that will keep me grounded, but I will be praying for you to hear your calling and for you to fulfill it."

Chris knew that only God could do the things that have taken place over the course of these events. The guard had listened intently while giving them more time that he was allowed as he watched Chris's impression of what was being said. It was clear that Chris was impressed with what this young man was saying and felt there was more to it than what meets the eye.

The court date rolled around, and Zach was presented before the judge, who declared him eligible to stand trial. There were questions being asked of him to decipher his actions regarding the witnesses that were allowed to escape. The judge wanted to know, was he aware that by releasing them it would possibly lead to his incarceration?

The explanation that Zach gave surprised the judge. It was disclosed that he didn't like killing people, it didn't make sense to him, he shot animals to eat, and he wasn't planning on eating any of those people.

This got a chuckle from the gallery but agitated the judge. The line of questioning continued from the judge, asking Zach if he was aware that his family members were shedding blood of innocent lives? His answer was simply, yes. The judge wanted him to elaborate, such heinous crimes needed to be somehow understood by the public. As well as explain why he didn't stop them?

"The only way to stop them would have been to kill them. Now, I wasn't wanting to kill my only kinfolk. I allowed those people to escape, to find help, in hopes that they'd get caught by the police, and put an end to the killing. But it didn't seem that anybody was interested in catching us. It was like a long nightmare. That's not on me, that's on them that didn't take action. Besides, if I stood up against Ma, she would have shot me. Then I wouldn't be able to carry out God's will."

"God's will? What are you talking about?" The judge was confused by his remarks.

"I have an assignment, I thought I told you that before."

"Just what kind of assignment are you on, young man?"

"An assignment to spread the Gospel, sir."

"Gospel?"

"Yes sir, the Good News, that Jesus came to demonstrate God's love for us. He died so that we can go home one day."

"You won't be going home for a long time, young man."

Zach knew he didn't understand what he was trying to share. The judge had paused trying to make sense of what he was saying. He was back to thinking this young man was not fully cognitive of his faculties.

"So, you are saying that you have been given this assignment directly from God?"

"Yes sir, Jesus Himself."

He went on to witness to the judge and any that were listening about his experiences, assuming he had not read all about his incident. Starting with how Chris Chaplain witnessed to him, how he met Jesus in heaven, and was sent back to complete His purpose on earth. Explaining that Jesus said that he was supposed to be an evangelist, and now he has that opportunity to fulfill it behind bars.

Zach was unleashed, words just kept flowing from him that captivated his audience, including the judge because he would usually not allow a defendant to carry on this way. People from outside the courtroom started coming in to listen to Zach's testimony. Before long the courtroom was packed.

People were texting others about the killer that met Jesus. The court attendants were turning people away, there was no room for the numbers that were showing curiosity. It got the attention of the media, who were now lining up to capture some of his testimony on the television.

It didn't bother Zach in the least, the more that heard the Good News the better. He went on to share that in Christ he was blessed, preselected, and chosen for his assignment. God accepted him as he was and adopted him into His family. He explained how he was redeemed and forgiven.

Then he looked out at all the faces staring at him. "You can find that for yourselves throughout the Word, just read about it in Ephesians, all that you are needing to draw you to Him, is this here book, called the Bible." He held it up for all to see.

Chris and Ellen were seated in the courtroom cheering him on with their smiles of joy.

Zach looked straight at the judge and quoted Romans 8:14-17 (NIV). "*For those who are led by the Spirit of God are the children of God. The Spirit you received does not make you slaves, so that you live in fear again; rather, the Spirit you received brought about your adoption to sonship, And by him we cry, 'Abba, Father.' The Spirit himself testified with our spirit that we are God's children. Now if we are children then we are heirs—heirs of God and co-heirs with Christ, if indeed we share in his sufferings in order that we may also share in his glory.'*"

"Young man, I don't know what you are trying to pull here, but it wasn't a good spirit that was calling you to be a part of those killings. The suffering part will be on you."

"Sir, I didn't know Jesus before I died." He stated flatly but not disrespectfully.

"What? You died and now you are standing in my courtroom?" The judge thought this absurd. Zach thought he had not been listening.

"Yes sir. I'm sure there are those who can give a testimony to my dying, and I am now standing here."

This information was blowing the mind of the judge, it was time to take a break, and he wanted some more information about what was going on in his courtroom. What was this kid talking about? Dying and now living? Talking to Jesus. And why was his courtroom filling up with so many stragglers. The judge even called the guard that had been watching over Zach to come to his office to see if he could enlighten him on anything that Zach had said behind bars. Was he trying to play the courts? Was this all going on to just get attention? Was he different behind the bars of a jail cell?

Ellen and Chris were amazed at what was happening in the courtroom. The sheer numbers of people that were flocking in to hear Zach's testimony had to be an act of God. They saw the media there and thought how Zach's story was to be told over national news. God meant for a message to get out.

They were a little worried about the judge and his attitude towards Zach but appreciated that he was allowing him the freedom to talk versus shutting him down. They would have to wait and see what his reaction would be when the court adjourned again. Chris had given Zach a thumbs up when he walked past him. Wanting to encourage him and for him to keep a positive attitude.

What was not revealed to them at the time was that large numbers could mean trouble. Numbers draw greater attention to the case. People will form varying opinions of what is being said in the courtroom and spin it into their own justice with their words. Most will be seeking justice for those who died and the one on trial right now was, Zach. Jasper was already dead, so they will be looking for someone to take the fall for all the deaths.

Louise had her own case coming up, but she, being the master of deception, could sway the jurors into thinking that it was Zach who was the mastermind behind it all. Jesus had warned Zach that things could get rocky. Zach was prepared, but Chris and Ellen had no idea what was about to unfold.

The judge had heard from various people in his chambers regarding Zach. He had people come from his hometown to give an account of what they thought of Zach as a young man. The guard was spoken to that had Zach's detail. The paramedics and police on the scene of the accident were brought in to discuss what they had witnessed. He even brought in Chris and talked with him, seeing how his name was brought up and he was the victim in this case. All of which would come out further in the trial considering he and his family were all surviving victims in the most recent account.

Based on what he was hearing, he did believe that Zach had good intentions behind his actions and what he was sharing in his courtroom. It was revealed that he had been misled by his family. The way the judge was reading it, apparently, he had either snapped from the stress, or he had a true conversion. The medics could not explain his recovery from being shot, this miracle was too much for the judge to process, so he decided to leave that one alone.

The fact remained that Zach still needed to stand trial for his part in the looting and ransacking of people's homes and the discharging of a weapon in the direction of individuals.

The court case continued over several days, and curiosity continued to grow among the people. The news media hyped the story and got people a little bloodthirsty, they love to twist a story to suit them getting larger numbers.

This was not the outcome Chris and Ellen were hoping for. People were swarming the courtroom like sharks after blood in the water. Even though his attorney brought the survivors forward to testify how Zach had not been the one to shoot to kill. Again, things were being twisted to the point some thought their testimony may have hurt Zach, more than helped, because they were clearly stating that he did fire upon them. It became a slippery slope.

Zach remained calm through the process until they brought his mother in to testify against him. He didn't see that one coming. To hear her state such lies against him unnerved him. It was a stab in his heart.

The verse that surfaced Zach's memory was, "*You shall not bear false witness against your neighbor* (Exodus 20:16 NKJV)." Well, how about against your own son? Had his mother not been warned, "*A false witness will not go unpunished, And he who speaks lies shall perish* (Proverbs 19:9 NKJV)."

The day would come when he would have to testify against her, but he was not going to give a false testimony, he was only going to state what was true about his mother and about her manipulation of her sons. Time may be needed to heal from this betrayal of his mother, but he knew that when he had the opportunity, he would witness to her what forgiveness looked like.

The verdict came down and Zach was sentenced to ten years in prison. The judge gave Zach an opportunity to speak, and he was prepared to give his final statement to all those who had been mocking him and wishing the worst-case scenario for him. He was prepared for prison, after all, that's where his mission field was, what he wasn't expecting was the ridicule that he had to endure through this process in the courtroom.

Zach stood and opened his Bible for all to see. "*May those who seek my life be disgraced and put to shame; may those who plot my ruin be turned back in dismay. May they be like chaff before the wind, with the angel of the*

LORD driving them away; may their path be dark and slippery, with the angel of the LORD pursuing them.

Since they hid their net for me without cause and without cause dug a pit for me, may ruin overtake them by surprise—may the net they hid entangle them, may they fall into the pit, to their ruin. Then my soul will rejoice in the LORD and delight in his salvation. My whole being will exclaim, 'Who is like you, LORD? You rescue the poor from those too strong for them, the poor and needy from those who rob them.

Ruthless witnesses come forward; they question me on things I know nothing about. They repay me evil for good and leave me like one bereaved. Yet when they were ill, I put on sackcloth and humbled myself with fasting. When my prayers returned to me unanswered, I went about mourning as though for my friend or brother. I bowed my head in grief as though weeping for my mother. But when I stumbled, they gathered in glee; assailants gathered against me without my knowledge. They slandered me without ceasing. Like the ungodly they maliciously mocked; they gnashed their teeth at me.

How long, Lord, will you look on? Rescue me from their ravages, my precious life from these lions. I will give you thanks in the great assembly; among the throngs I will praise you. Do not let those gloat over me who are my enemies without cause; do not let those who hate me without reason maliciously wink the eye. They do not speak peaceably, but devise false accusations against those who live quietly in the land. They sneer at me and say, 'Aha! Aha! With our own eyes we have seen it.'

LORD, you have seen this; do not be silent. Do not be far from me, Lord. Awake, and rise to my defense! Contend for me, my God and Lord. Vindicate me in your righteousness, LORD my God; do not let them gloat over me. (Psalm 35:4-24 NIV).'"

The papers would have a heyday with that, but they would have to recite the Scripture in public view and that pleased Zach.

Song "Eye of The Storm" by Ryan Stevenson

11

HOSPITALITY

The hospitality of Miss Mae had been a huge help and relief to Chris and Ellen during the court proceedings. They had accepted her offer to stay with her and they were amenable to her accommodations and assistance. But they insisted on doing their part, Ellen handled the shopping and provided the groceries needed for all of them. Chris put his skills to use mending the chicken coop, and the loose boards on the front porch. Pop helped in the garden while taking care of Elsie.

Miss Mae loved every minute of their stay, if it was up to her, she'd have them with her all the time. God had provided her with companionship to take away some of her loneliness, but she knew that it wouldn't last.

Their stay ended up being longer than they expected, and due to the length of the court case a hotel room would have wiped out their budget. They were given a small stipend for their inconvenience, but it would not have allowed for as comfortable a stay as the accommodations provided by Miss Mae, which was a win-win for everyone.

Arrangements had to be made to push back their work schedules, there would be a lapse in job production from Chris, which would lead to a loss of income. It was a good thing that they had savings set aside for a rainy day. They just never thought that it was going to rain this long. Miss Mae's hospitality was greatly appreciated.

They were too deeply involved in this court case to leave town. They didn't want to miss anything that was being said or done. They were invested in the outcome of this case. After all, they were the victims of a heinous crime, threatened to be killed, yet with all the tragedy, they witnessed a miracle of God, not one that any of them would ever forget. Would they not want to see how it all played out? It would not have been on the news back home, so, to stay abreast of things, they had to be there.

George was enjoying the newfound friendship of Miss Mae as well; he hadn't realized how much he missed the everyday little occurrences that are experienced with a companion, and conversations over a cup of coffee. He had friends at home to keep him busy, but they included events or activities that were scheduled, it was these simple moments that he missed having with his wife. And he was ever so grateful to Miss Mae for not having to be holed up in a hotel room somewhere with Elsie.

Being an active child, she would have become easily bored, the confinement of one room consisting of four walls would have closed in on them quickly. Here she had the great outdoors to play in with plenty to do alongside Miss Mae. Who was teaching her how to collect eggs from the chickens. Pearl did her part in keeping Elsie entertained for the most part inside, and Miss Mae had her helping in the kitchen setting the table, drying dishes, and even learning to do a little cooking. They found plenty to keep Elsie busy and engaged.

When Chris and Ellen would return from the court proceedings for the day, it was time to recap everything for George and Miss Mae over a cup of afternoon tea. They were free to speak their minds after having to keep their peace in the courtroom.

Chris was angry over how they were spinning the truth and trying to make out like Zach was demented, demented enough to coordinate the thefts and killing spree all on his own. Now that was far from reality.

"Have they never heard Exodus 23:1 (NASB) before, '*You shall not bear a false report; do not join your hand with a wicked man to be a malicious witness. You shall not follow the masses in doing evil, nor shall you testify in a dispute so as to turn aside after a multitude in order to pervert justice.*' They are perverting justice, plain and simple. And what about the fact that they are upsetting the Lord as well, look only to Zechariah 8:17 (NASB), '*Let none of you devise evil in your heart against another, and do not love perjury; for all these are what I hate, 'declares the LORD.*' The Lord hates perjury, I tell you." He was infuriated.

"Honey, God has spoken, *'A false witness will not go unpunished. And he who speaks lies will not escape* (Proverbs 19:5 NKJV).' I guess lawyers don't follow the laws of God, just the laws written from man. It's obvious that they are twisting truths around to suit them, but they won't get away with it."

"I can't wait until it's my turn on the stand. I will give them all something to think about. They will hear what Proverbs 25:18 (NASB) says, *'Like a club and a sword and a sharp arrow is a man who bears false witness against his neighbor.'* But I'm going to come down on them like a club with the Word. These lawyers are as guilty as Zach's mother. Apparently, they haven't heard Jesus speak on the subject of commandments that should be kept in order to enter into life. Matthew 19:18 (NKJV) spells it out for them, *'He said to Him, 'Which ones?' Jesus said, 'You shall not murder, You shall not commit adultery, You shall not steal, You shall not bear false witness.'* And yet they allowed Zach's mother to get away with all of that. I'm sorry if I'm sounding a bit redundant, but this just flies all over me."

"Chris, we have to remember that Zach is not going to be freed of all his charges, he will go to jail. That's part of the Lord's plan for him. That's where he wants to go, it's his mission field, you've heard him talk about it. He is passionate about serving the Lord and he recognizes that he is taking hope into the prison."

"You're right, I'm just afraid for him. But what we must pray against, is that the lies don't get him a death penalty." Thinking the worst from all the hype that has been playing out.

"You don't think it would come to that, do you?" George desired accountability for the stress and anguish they were all put through, but he recognized that Zach had a transformation, and that he was now on a mission from God. He didn't want the death penalty any more than his kids did.

"I believe they are out for blood. They will be pushing for the death penalty for Zach, because they don't want to execute a woman."

Elsie walked in at that moment and asked what that meant. They each looked at the other one and were hesitant to answer her question. What took them by surprise was Miss Mae's answer.

"When someone has done something really bad and has stood before a judge to be punished, sometimes that punishment means they lose their life. It's a system of justice."

Elsie was shocked and upset that Zach might lose his life. Bowing her sweet little head asking that they all pray together and ask that Zach receives the help he needs. Chris smiled at his daughter and thought, out of the mouth of a child, yes, prayer is what is needed. They held hands and Chris led them in prayer.

"Dear Lord, Zach may be in a fight for his life. You are the one who gave him life to serve you. May you not forget him now in his time of need. You have written, '*You will not have to fight this battle. Take up your positions; stand firm and see the deliverance the LORD will give you, Judah and Jerusalem. Do not be afraid; do not be discouraged. Go out to face them tomorrow, and the LORD will be with you* (2 Chronicles 20:17 NIV).' You have stated in Psalm 107:6 (NIV), '*Then they cried out to the LORD in their trouble, and he delivered them from their distress.*' You have done it before, and we know that you can do it again."

Chris leaned down and picked up the Bible and flipped to Psalm 34 and began to read a passage that he felt he was led to, that fit their situation.

"'*The angel of the LORD encamps around those who fear him, and he delivers them. Taste and see that the LORD is good; blessed is the one who takes refuge in him. Fear the LORD, you his holy people, for those who fear him lack nothing. The lions may grow weak and hungry, but those who seek the LORD lack no good thing.*

Come, my children, listen to me; I will teach you the fear of the LORD. Whoever of you loves life and desires to see many good days, keep your tongue from evil and your lips from telling lies. Turn from evil and do good; seek peace and pursue it. The eyes of the LORD are on the righteous, and his ears are attentive to their cry; but the face of the LORD is against those who do evil, to blot out their name from the earth. The righteous cry out, and the LORD hears them; he delivers them from all their troubles. The LORD is close to the brokenhearted and saves those who are crushed in spirit. The righteous person may have many troubles, but the LORD delivers him from them all (Psalm 34:7-19 NIV).'"

"Honey, that was the perfect message for us. I feel the Lord led you to that passage."

Miss Mae popped up, not wanting to forget her manners. She after all was playing hostess.

"Those lions may go hungry, but I'm not letting you all go hungry. I'll agree with the Word that you won't lack for anything. We have been busy in the kitchen all day. Now, let's eat."

Miss Mae was eager to feed them, she had been cooking all afternoon with Elsie's help and she knew they would be ready for some nourishment, so she had prepared a feast for them.

Song "Better Days Coming" by MercyMe

12

TEA PARTY

They had been so caught up in the trial that they had forgotten about Elsie's little routines. She had already missed a few of her tea times from all the disruptions going on and she thought it was very important that she have tea with Jesus this Friday. She discussed it with Miss Mae who said she would be pleased to set a table for tea.

Although she was under the impression she was setting up a playtime tea for Elsie, she still pulled out all the stops for the finest tea setting. Spreading her fine linen tablecloth out on the dining table, along with her fancy sterling silver tea service. Considering Elsie had done without for so many weeks, she felt this teatime should be special. She was busy in the kitchen preparing little tea cookies and a bowl of raspberries, along with small finger sandwiches from leftover chicken salad.

Elsie had run outside to pick some wildflowers for the table. Pop assisted her in getting a vase and water for the flowers, it had become a real group effort. Elsie placed her flowers in the center of the table and was very pleased with the arrangement on the table as she stood back to inspect things. She looked up at Miss Mae smiling and telling her how Jesus will be so pleased. Miss Mae did not get the connection that the tea party was actually for Jesus, she just assumed it was something sweet Elsie stated as a way of saying thank you.

Elsie sat at the table saying a little prayer, when she suddenly stopped, looked up and asked Pop if he thought Jesus would know where they were. Pop assured Elsie that Jesus always knew where to find them.

"*'The LORD watches over all who love him* (Psalm 143:20 NIV). *From heaven the LORD looks down and sees all mankind; from his dwelling place he watches all who live on earth* (Psalm 33:13,14 NIV).' So yes, sweet girl, He knows exactly where you are."

That pleased Elsie and she went back to her prayers as Pop and Miss Mae left the room to have coffee in the kitchen instead of tea with Elsie. Elsie sat waiting patiently on Jesus to arrive for tea. She turned to Pearl, who had made an appearance hoping to nibble on some chicken salad. Stating happily to Pearl that Jesus would arrive soon, and she would introduce her if she stayed for tea.

It wasn't long before Elsie was chatting with Jesus and the introductions commenced. Jesus was pleased to have Pearl as an extra guest and noted that she had become a sweet companion for Elsie, who was apologizing for not having Him over for tea sooner. Expressing how glad she was that He found her at Miss Mae's house, as she was pointing out the lovely table that Miss Mae had set for them. Continuing on about how it was much nicer than her toy tea set, and then she whispered that it was real tea. Giggling commenced.

Elsie proceeded to tell Him all about Zach and what she had overheard from her parents. It had upset her, and she knew that Jesus would know what to do about it.

Jesus replied, "*'If you remain in me and my words remain in you, ask whatever you wish, and it will be done for you* (John 15:7 NIV).'"

"I don't want Zach to die." Elsie said with a tender heart.

Jesus was trying to explain that He was watching over Zach and that he had been given a commission, a special assignment. "*'Everyone who calls on the name of the Lord will be saved. How, then, can they call on the one they have not believed in? And how can they believe in the one of whom they have not heard? And how can they hear without someone preaching to them? And how can anyone preach unless they are sent? As it is written; 'How beautiful are the feet of those who bring good news!* (Romans 10:13-15 NIV).'"

There was a lot being said that Elsie didn't follow but she trusted Jesus and knew that He knew best, even if His explanation was not clear to her.

Jesus looked at sweet Elsie's confused face and answered her with a simple explanation in a comforting tone, that Zach wouldn't die until he had completed the task of delivering the Good News to those who haven't heard of Him. Once that's completed then He would take him home.

"Home? Where is his home?" Elsie asked, not knowing anything about Zach, really, except that her parents cared about him, as she did too.

Again, His answers had to be put in terms she would understand, defining home was with Him, in heaven where He prepares a home for everyone that knows Him. Making it clear that one day when each person is ready, they will be with Him.

With all smiles Elsie shared what she knew. "Like my grandma, she is in heaven."

Jesus confirmed that she certainly was and that she was very proud of her.

"Does she see me?" she asked with excitement.

This was an opportunity for Jesus to impart a little knowledge about heaven to her as He explained that on her birthday her grandmother was able to look down and send her special blessings from heaven. This would be something that He shares with her when she is a little older and can take her to the portal where the saints are given an opportunity to observe their loved ones.

"When I visit heaven, can I go see her?" She was being inquisitive, now.

The seed had been planted; Elsie was grasping the fact that she would be visiting heaven on a regular basis. This pleased Jesus and He was able to share that she would be revealing a lot of things about heaven to others. That was to be her assignment, just like Zach has an assignment for Him in the prison. That topic had not been finished for Elsie.

"Will he stay there a long time?"

There was more of an indirect answer given as it was pointed out that it wouldn't seem like a long time to him. Revealing that when one is serving a purpose for a higher good, then time doesn't seem as important as one would think.

This didn't really make sense to her, but she was so full of questions that she carried on without digging deeper into any specific meaning. Jesus was always happy to try and answer her questions. He was building a strong foundation in their relationship.

"Will he be okay there?"

After making it clear that He would always be with Zach, Jesus changed course in the conversation wanting to leave her with a message for her father.

"Okay."

This was something new for her, she was going to get to deliver a message from Jesus to her daddy. She felt like a big girl with an important task and was eager to know what she was to deliver. It all seemed pretty easy to her at first. She just needed to convey that they weren't to worry, and that Zach was going where he needed to be. Then Jesus gave her a verse to remember to give to her father, this seemed a little more difficult, but Jesus had her repeat Exodus 7:3 back to Him to ensure her she could do it.

"Exodus 7:3, got it." Pleased with herself that she remembered.

Jesus smiled at her and thanked her for the lovely tea, and then He was gone.

Elsie continued to enjoy her tea with Pearl as if this was an everyday occurrence. Pop and Miss Mae overheard parts of Elsie's side of the conversation, yet they believed she was having a conversation with herself. Although it didn't much sound like a normal kid's discussion. She had been talking about heaven, her grandma, and Exodus 7:3. What concerned them was the poor little thing was still concerned about Zach.

When she came into the kitchen for more tea, she was asked who she was talking to other than Pearl.

She looked around the room confused by their question, then answered, "Jesus."

"Jesus? Are you sure?" asked Pop.

"Yes, I have tea with Jesus on Fridays." she said matter-of-factly. "Although it was nice to have Pearl join us today." Having been pleased with the extra guest.

"What does Jesus look like, dear?" Miss Mae asked out of curiosity.

"He looks like Jesus. He has a nice smile."

Pop and Miss Mae agreed that they would need to share this event with Chris and Ellen when they got home. Neither one of them knew exactly how to deal with her imagination.

Song "You Are God Alone" by Rikki Doolan

13

SENTENCING

The court date finally arrived. Chris had his day in court and shared on behalf of the family what they had witnessed and experienced. Trying to put a more positive spin on things. He had his opportunity to confirm what Zach had been saying, after all he was an eyewitness to everything. It was his time to speak boldly about what other witnesses had stated and to confront the narrative of the prosecutors who had twisted the events and spoken untruths. He knew that Zach was not the hardened criminal that the prosecutors made him out to be.

Trying to be clear that who they were prosecuting was a misguided youth that was threatened and drugged alongside his family, to commit crimes that he did not have a heart for. It was shared that he saw the light that was truly in Zach and had shared the Gospel with him, Jesus had stepped in and handled the rest. Proceeding with the perspective of the miracle that he witnessed, Zach was dead without life in his body and then he was resurrected before their eyes.

Chris went on to say, "Since his miracle, he has not been the same man. The man you have seen before you, testifying, changed when he saw Jesus, and wishes to do good. How can you sentence him for the sins of his family? Jesus saved this man, don't be the ones that put him to death." Chris was pleading for his life.

There had been conflicting truths presented, and it was on purpose by the prosecution to confuse the jurors. They were trying to get in the last word that would lay heavy on the jurors' hearts before making a final verdict.

Chris had hoped that his testimony would have weight, considering the fact that he was the victim, and was wanting a best-case scenario for Zach. Yes, he would serve time and be held accountable for his part, but he was hopeful that it would not be in a hardened prison, and that they would be lenient on the sentencing, most importantly he didn't want them to take his life.

Once again, Zach was given an opportunity to speak before the court and he was prepared, Bible in hand, he opened it up to the verses he wanted to share in hopes that it would make a difference. Some would see it as a staged event to get sympathy, anything to avoid the death penalty. Zach just wanted to share truth.

"*Have mercy on me, O God, according to your unfailing love; according to your great compassion blot out my transgressions. Wash away all my iniquity and cleanse me from my sin. For I know my transgressions, and my sin is always before me. Against you, you only, have I sinned and done what is evil in your sight; so you are right in your verdict and justified when you judge. Surely I was sinful at birth, sinful from the time my mother conceived me. Yet you desired faithfulness even in the womb; you taught me wisdom in that secret place.*

Cleanse me with hyssop, and I will be clean; wash me, and I will be whiter than snow. Let me hear joy and gladness; let the bones you have crushed rejoice. Hide your face from my sins and blot out all my iniquity. Create in me a pure heart, O God, and renew a steadfast spirit within me. Do not cast me from your presence or take your Holy Spirit from me. Restore to me the joy of your salvation and grant me a willing spirit, to sustain me. Then I will teach transgressors your ways, so that sinners will turn back to you. Deliver me from the guilt of bloodshed, O God, you who are God my Savior, and my tongue will sing of your righteousness (Psalm 50:1-14 NIV).'"

Zach shut the Bible with great reverence and continued. "God is surely with me to have pointed me into the Word that best expresses my heart. He alone, I seek to please. He has given me an assignment to teach the Word to those who need hope, so where you send me is where my mission field will be. And the Lord will guide and sustain me."

The judge just seemed to be aggravated with Zach's final remarks. He had the choice of what prison to send Zach to and chose the harshest one out of spite. Zach's attorney was floored with his decision and promised to try his best to get him moved from that facility.

Zach wasn't showing fear until he witnessed the concern from his attorney. He had no idea of one prison from the next. Most of his time, to this point, had been in a jail cell. He really wasn't sure what he was getting into. Yet he continued to trust in the Lord.

Chris leaned over the rail trying to encourage Zach, he only had a minute to speak to him before they whisked him off to prison. "2 Thessalonians 3:3 (NASB), *'The Lord is faithful, and He will strengthen and protect you from the evil one.'* And in this case, he will protect you from the worst of prisons."

Ellen wanted to say something to Zach, knowing that it could be the last time she saw him for a long time, but the words wouldn't come out clearly through the tears and sobs. She settled for a hug over the rail, until the guard snatched him back and removed him from the courtroom. It was just a prelude as to what life was going to be like.

There wasn't any way to console Ellen, she was sad and angry at the judge. Yes, the jurors found him guilty, but it was the judge who sentenced him to that prison, a despicable place. Did he not recognize the fact that Zach was a new creation in Jesus? He was a new man. She couldn't wrap her mind around it.

The judge had heard their testimony, the testimony of all the witnesses, he heard Zach's testimony, and he still showed no mercy. Chris assured her that the attorney was going to try everything to get him out of that prison.

They agreed that they would not discuss this outcome at Miss Mae's in front of Elsie. It was not necessary to upset their little girl. They were afraid that she may have overheard more than she should have, already.

When they arrived back at Miss Mae's, they both had a worried look on their face, reflecting the outcome of the day. Pop just came out with it and asked if it was the death penalty. They shook their heads, no, but before they could say anything else, Miss Mae spoke up and told them they needed to wipe that look off their faces before Elsie saw them. Explaining that she was already upset about Zach and their look would frighten her. Of course, that caused them even more concern, but they knew she was right.

"Has she said something?" Ellen was now worried about Elsie.

"Well, she had a rather unusual afternoon." Miss Mae stated.

"What do you mean?" Chris was now a bit anxious to hear what they had to say about Elsie's day.

"I helped her prepare for a little tea party, and it's the conversation that she had by herself that was so unusual."

"She loves her tea party time with Jesus. I'm afraid we have kept her from that for a while, with all that has been going on. I'm sure she had a lovely time; you were so kind to set it up for her."

"Yes, that's all fine, but are you aware that she apparently talks with Jesus?"

Ellen nodded and smiled as if everything was normal. "Yes, she chats with Him a lot."

"Like she is having a real conversation." Miss Mae insisted, with big, confused eyes. She was convinced something unusual was going on.

"Yes, she's fine. She has a special gift; I'll have to explain more later. I'm just so tired after the verdict today. I want to hug my baby girl and lay down a while."

Miss Mae knew that Elsie was special, but she was unsure of what Ellen was talking about, when she stated she had a special gift. No need to probe right now, she knew it had been a long, hard day.

There were other things to be concerned with. Now that the court case was completed, they would be leaving her soon. This left Miss Mae with her own sadness to deal with. She had grown accustomed to having them around. Would they come and visit her? Would they forget about her?

Elsie came running into the room grabbing her daddy's legs. "I have a message for you."

"What is it sweetie?" He picked her up and looked into her excited eyes.

"Jesus said, don't worry, Zach is going where he is supposed to go. And, and 3,7." She knew she had forgotten something she was supposed to have remembered.

"3 and 7, What does that mean, sweetie?" He knew he was missing something out of that message.

Elsie looked confused, and a bit upset. She thought she had remembered it correctly. Her dad was supposed to know what it meant. Pop had overheard her state it before, during the tea party, so he joined in on the conversation to correct her.

"I believe you said Exodus 7:3." He had not looked it up, but he remembered what was recited by Elsie.

"That's right, did you hear Jesus too?" she asked with enthusiasm.

"No baby girl, but I heard you repeat that to Him." He smiled big at his precious grandchild not fully comprehending what was going on with her tea parties.

Chris reached for the Bible and turned to Exodus 7:3 (NASB) and read it aloud getting everyone's attention. "*But I will harden Pharoah's heart that I may multiply My signs and My wonders in the land of Egypt.*" What does that mean?"

"It's our answer." Ellen stated with excitement. "We asked why the judge was so harsh. Jesus is telling us that He hardened his heart for His purposes." Ellen was suddenly feeling much better about the day.

How rewarding it was to hear from the Lord. The message must have been delivered before they even knew the direction that Zach was headed, and their questions were asked. Ellen was amazed at how great her God was. Yet He is a God of the past, present, and future all in one as stated in Hebrews 13:8, and Malachi 3:6 (NKJV) clearly states, "*For I am the LORD, I do not change.*"

Still a little taken aback by the prison facility selected for Zach to be taken to. His life could be in danger there. It also presented a problem that it would be so far away that it would be hard for him to visit.

Chris was aware that Zach was not just serving a sentence, he was serving the Lord, but he will now have to watch his back even more closely, in order to stay alive. Chris would have to take comfort in the knowledge that if this is where the Lord meant for him to be, then there is a reason for it. He was grateful for the message from the Lord. It did bring comfort to Ellen and Chris.

Song "New Creation" by Mac Powell

14

PRISON

"Do not be anxious about anything, but in every situation, by prayer and petition, with thanksgiving, present your requests to God. And the peace of God, which transcends all understanding, will guard your hearts and your minds in Christ Jesus. Finally, brothers and sisters, whatever is true, whatever is noble, whatever is right, whatever is pure, whatever is lovely, whatever is admirable—if anything is excellent or praiseworthy—think about such things. Whatever you have learned or received or heard from me, or seen in me—put it into practice. And the God of peace will be with you (Philippians 4:6-9 NIV)."

Zach reflected on this Scripture to guard his heart as he was being processed into the prison. Grateful that he had been allowed to keep his Bible with him. His nose was forever in the pages, pouring over the Word to find comfort and messaging for others that he came into contact with.

The surroundings were enough to cause dread in anyone's heart. Yet, he knew he was not alone; the presence of Jesus was felt, and it strengthened him. Realizing that his focus needed to be kept on Jesus and what He had shared with him while he was in heaven, and not to be discouraged with his surroundings.

What came to mind was the story of Peter, it was as if Jesus was speaking to him and showing him where to find encouragement. How Peter was able to walk on the water, as long as he kept his focus on Jesus. It was a reminder that Jesus is the one who gives us the ability to accomplish our goals.

When Peter focused on Jesus, he was able to stay above the water, but when he took his eyes off Jesus and focused on the storm, he sunk into the depths. Zach was aware of the importance to stay focused, keep his eye on the prize, his mission for Jesus, and he would be fine. He would not get distracted by the enemy that may cause chaos around him, nor the depressing facility he found himself in. Jesus would be with him to lift him up and help him solve whatever problem came his way.

The backup plan that he clung to was that there was an assurance that he had a reserved place in heaven, should any harm come to him. He knew where he would be going. There was no fear of death, just maybe the difficulties that may arise. Jesus laid on Zach's heart, the right Scripture for him to rest in, and to rejoice in. Not fully aware of what authority he carried, but in due time it would be revealed to him.

"Behold, I have given you authority to tread on serpents and scorpions, and over all the power of the enemy, and nothing will injure you. Nevertheless do not rejoice in this, that the spirits are subject to you, but rejoice that your names are recorded in heaven (Luke 10:19,20 NASB)."

Once Zach got settled in his cell, the cellmate informed him that talk had spread throughout the prison, about his case. It was amazing to find out how quickly news spread in a jail, this may be to his advantage when he shared the Gospel. Zach was trying to find the positive in all things. The cellmate, Joe, warned him that some might want to challenge him. They had heard that he died and came back to life. Some were inclined to kill him to see if it would happen again. It was as if they were making him a sport. A game that he was not interested in playing.

Zach outlined a little about his assignment from heaven, how he was there to motivate them, to get them serious about God. If they tried anything, he felt sure that Jesus would protect him, because he was assured that Jesus was watching over him wanting him to have success spreading the Good News.

Turning to his cellmate thanking him for the warning, then reciting Romans 12:12 (NIV). "*Be joyful in hope, patient in affliction, faithful in prayer.*"

His cellmate was intrigued about the quote. "How are you to be patient about suffering? That makes no sense. I don't think you have experienced what they can do to you in here."

"No, but I'm strengthened by the Word, let's see what else the Bible has to say."

Opening the Bible up to the exact place that Jesus would have taken him to, Romans 12 and he began to read. "'*Bless those who persecute you; bless and do not curse. Rejoice with those who rejoice, and weep with those who weep. Be of the same mind toward one another; do not be haughty in mind, but associate with the lowly. Do not be wise in your own estimation. Never pay back evil for evil to anyone. Respect what is right in the sight of all men. If possible, so far as it depends on you, be at peace with all men. Never take your own revenge, beloved, but leave room for the wrath of God, for it is written, 'VENGEANCE IS MINE, I WILL REPAY,' says the Lord. Do not be overcome by evil, but overcome evil with good* (Romans 12:14-19,21 NASB).'"

"Well, that's a mouthful you got there, Zach. But you will soon know who to respect in here. And it might bring you some peace, if they side with you." Joe delivered a warning with advice.

"I appreciate your advice." Zach was confident who was on his side, so he wasn't as concerned as he possibly needed to be.

Zach settled into his bunk, excited about his first opportunity to introduce the Bible to someone who actually asked about it. There was an overwhelming feeling that he was in the right place to complete his work. He continued to share with this young man, Joe, that he was new to the Bible himself, and that they could study it together, to see where it led them in understanding. He felt sure the Holy Spirit would guide them to truths. His story captivated the young man, letting Zach know that he would have his back, as long as they were assigned together.

It was an undeniable fact that Jesus handpicked his roommate. There was a great amount of relief felt on Zach's part. As he was being shown the ropes of prison life, he portrayed himself as a confident man, how else could you present yourself when you have first-hand knowledge of what you are talking about. What he had to share was what people were drawn to. Many were interested in hearing Zach's story and along with it, his message for them.

Zach was sharing his story through the written Word, "'*I waited patiently for the LORD; And He inclined to me and heard my cry. He brought me up out of the pit of destruction, out of the miry clay, And He set my feet upon a rock making my footsteps firm. He put a new song in my mouth, a song of praise to our God; Many will see and fear And will trust in the LORD. How blessed is the man who has made the LORD his trust. And has not turned to the proud, nor to those who lapse into falsehood. Many, O LORD my God, are the wonders which You have done, And Your thoughts toward us; there is none to compare with You. If I would declare and speak of them, They would be too numerous to count* (Psalm 40:1-5 NASB).'"

Thinking that this verse fit his life, explaining that it could apply to them as well. What really got their attention was when he went on to share about his miracle, that he was dead, and saw his body from heaven, yet Jesus wanted him to come and speak to them about His great love for them. That it's not too late for them to seek Jesus. There were questions about his experiences in heaven that drew a lot of them into discussion, which pleased him.

Zach continued to speak boldly to the ones who wanted to listen. "'*The Spirit of the Lord is on me, because he has anointed me to proclaim good news to the poor. He has sent me to proclaim freedom for the prisoners and recovery of sight for the blind, to set the oppressed free* (Luke 4:18 NIV).' These words were written for another, but they are true today as well. The Words in the Bible are living Words from the past, for the present, and future. Just as our God is forever, unchanging. It is written, '*But you remain the same, and your years will never end. The children of your servants will live in your presence; their descendants will be established before you* (Psalm 102:27,28 NIV).'"

He was hoping he was getting their attention, although their focus seemed to be on the miracle part of his story.

"Open your hearts to hear what I have to say about the Lord who loves you and has sent me here to help you see Him, even in the midst of a prison cell. Don't fumble around in this darkness that is holding you captive, proclaim your freedom through Jesus Christ, who died for you. Hear what the Word in Psalm 32 has to say to you because it is meant for you."

The Bible was held up for all to see, then he turned to the Psalm and stated again firmly, "This Word is for you."

Then he read with conviction, "'*How blessed is he whose transgression is forgiven, Whose sin is covered! How blessed is the man to whom the LORD does not impute iniquity, And in whose spirit there is no deceit! When I kept silent about my sin, my body wasted away Through my groaning all day long. For day and night Your hand was heavy upon me; My vitality was drained away as with the fever heat of summer. I acknowledged my sin to You, And my iniquity I did not hid; I said, 'I will confess my transgressions to the LORD.' And you forgave the guilt of my sin.*

Therefore let all the faithful pray to you while you may be found; surely the rising of the mighty waters will not reach them. You are my hiding place; you will protect me from trouble and surround me with songs of deliverance. I will instruct you and teach you in the way you should go; I will counsel you with my loving eye on you. Do not be like the horse or the mule, which have no understanding but must be controlled by bit and bridle or they will not come to you. Many are the woes of the wicked, but the LORD's unfailing love surrounds the one who trust him. Rejoice in the LORD and be glad, you righteous; sing, all you who are upright in heart! (Psalm 32:1-11 NIV)."

He wasn't finished, yet he could recite Proverbs 28:13(NASB) from memory as he laid the Bible down. "*He who conceals his transgressions will not prosper, But he who confesses and forsakes them will find compassion.*'"

More men, young and old who had been in prison for a long time, came around to hear what this young man was talking about. It was Zach's confidence that drew people close. Some knew a little of what he was stating because they had attended Bible studies in prison. Some attended just to get out of work detail, others attended because there was interest in what was being shared. Yet they had never heard of the things that Zach was sharing. They were interested in this man's testimony.

"*This is what the LORD says, he who made the earth, the LORD who formed it and established it—the LORD is his name: 'Call to me and I will answer you and tell you great and unsearchable things you do not know. I will bring health and healing to it; I will heal my people and will let them enjoy abundant peace and security. I will cleanse them from all the sin they have committed against me and will forgive all their sins of rebellion against me. Then this city will bring me renown, joy, praise and honor before all nations on earth that hear of all the good things I do for it; and they will be in awe and will tremble at the abundant prosperity and peace I provide for it* (Jeremiah 33:2,3,6,8,9 NIV)."

Looking into the eyes of those around him, his heart was softened. "The Lord desires to free you from your sin, to heal, to provide you peace of mind and give you the security that you are His. You just need to accept Him. This bondage you and I are in does not need to define us. Your choices put you here, but I've come to give you hope to free your minds to prepare you for a life outside of this prison and outside this existence. I've seen heaven and I know of its peace and contentment."

There were men that listened intently, ones that were looking for some compassion from humanity, that had not been found. They were there living out a long sentence in captivity, and understood the comment about the all-day groanings, desiring some kind of hope and deliverance from their misery.

Here was a man standing before them that was declaring that they could be forgiven and could find freedom, through a renewing of their minds, peace could be found. That there was a God that loved them.

Song "Nobody" by Casting Crown, ft Matthew West

15
THE ATTACK

A week had gone by without an incident of any kind which was encouraging. Zach was settling into his new normal. Joe had been with him, as promised, to give him some cover. As he had stated, "I have your back", which became more than a figure of speech.

Joe stood at his side, watching intently the moves of the men around them, literally protecting him from attack. The rumors had risen that there were some that wanted to challenge Zach. They, being a thug group, that ruled behind the bars, wanted to see if he would be rescued, or would he experience another death. It was all for sport. Who would save him this time?

Prisoners had their own system of authority and ways to communicate with each other. Even during a lockdown there were ways to get messages to each other. They even established payoffs to the guards, bribing them to set things up to work in their favor.

Which is what happened when Joe and Zach got separated. Zach pulled a clean-up detail that would put him alone with The Butcher, a lifer, who got his name by reputation, who wanted to test the security measures over Zach. Was it supernatural or just luck? He wasn't afraid of anything; it was all the others who were afraid of him.

The Butcher, known by his comrades as Butch, was a big man, who apparently worked out a lot. His muscles bulged and were enough to frighten any newcomer to the prison into submission. There was a pecking order in the prison and The Butcher was the top man, who at this moment was wanting to peck Zach down to size.

Zach took one look around and knew that he was about to face a difficult situation. Butch stepped out from behind the tall refrigerator unit and walked in Zach's direction with determination, as if he had something to prove.

"So, they say you are invincible, shall we test that?" as he flexed his muscles.

"I don't know what they are saying about me. But if you are asking if I can die, the answer would be, yes. I have died, yet I live now, to serve God." Zach stated confidently, yet his heart was pounding rapidly, assuming he was about to receive a pounding.

"Are you trying to confuse me, little man?" He didn't like the way Zach smarted back at him, at least that was his impression of his comment.

"Not at all. I was shot and killed. I died. I went to heaven and Jesus sent me back to serve Him, by helping people like yourself."

Zach was giving a quick testimony realizing that Butch was not interested in his story, just what he could prove was true or fabricated.

"Help me with what?" Butch didn't believe he needed any kind of help, especially from a young pup fresh behind bars.

"To know the love that God has for you. He loves all mankind. He realizes that people make mistakes and need help righting their wrongs. Jesus died for you, sacrificed his life for yours. His blood opens doors to heaven for you, so that you don't have to live out eternity in torment."

"I'm living there now. But it's my choice." He practically growled his response in hopes of frightening Zach.

"It may seem that way, this is a judgment for the choices you made, but it is not eternal torment where you will be cursed to experience unquenchable fire, weeping and gnashing of teeth, and left without any hope or peace. This is not that. Jesus wants to save you from that eternal fiery existence."

"So why did he send you, instead of coming Himself?"

"He is here. He is with me, always."

"Is He going to save you from what I have planned for you?" His eyes got big with delight about the torture he wanted Zach to experience from him.

"'*Who shall separate us from the love of Christ? Shall trouble or hardship or persecution or famine or nakedness or danger or sword? As it is written: 'For your sake we face death all day long; we are considered as sheep to be slaughtered.' No in all these things we are more than conquerors through him who loved us. For I am convinced that neither death nor life, neither angels nor demons, neither the present nor the future, nor any powers, neither height nor depth, nor anything else in all creation, will be able to separate us from the love of God that is in Christ Jesus our Lord* (Romans 8:35-39 NIV).'"

"Well, I plan to do some separating. I want to see what you are made of."

With those words he pulled out a shiv, a handmade knife used in prison, and thrust it towards Zach with a powerful force. Yet he missed his target. Butch found that hard to believe, there was no way that Zach moved that fast.

Zach was a bit surprised at first that he was missed. Butch pulled back and struck again, this time with more vengeance than before. Zach was able to swat his hand away and land a blow to his face that shook the man to his core. Zach had some skill at protecting himself from his own brother, but he was amazed at the degree of strength that was behind his own blow.

It was known that sometimes to get a bully's attention you had to fight back, stand your ground, therefore he wasn't shying away from this fight. He had hoped that by showing Butch he wasn't afraid of him, he would stand down, but it just fired Butch up into a fighting frenzy.

It wasn't a fair fight considering he didn't have a weapon, but he did have quick moves and apparently some newfound strength and power to his blow, which he thanked the Lord for. It was as if he had a sixth sense as to when and how to move free of Butch's attempts. There was a newfound ability to wear him down, then land a few good blows, to the point where Butch shook his head and walked away.

It was not Zach's day to die, he had an assignment to complete, was his thought, when suddenly he was jumped from behind by several men at the same time. Butch had not come alone. He may have thrown in the towel, but his purpose was not complete until Zach was crushed and made an example of.

Zach was garnering too much attention in the prison and Butch didn't like distractions that would defy his status. The unexpected happened. No matter how hard they hit and punched Zach, he would not die. Their efforts made him look like minced meat, when they finally gave up and left him, but he remained alive.

The guards came in and found him in a pool of his own blood. A sight that they had seen before. The guards assumed he was dead until he let out a mournful moan. After being taken to the infirmary to be patched up, they sent him back to his cell. Apparently, all his wounds were superficial, yet he suffered some remaining soreness that was a reminder that he had been through something. The key was that Jesus saw him through it, another testimony. The guards were amazed at the amount of blood and yet he was able to return to his cell the same day.

While the doctor tended his wounds, having heard about the amount of blood loss that occurred, he commented that he had never seen someone recover from an attack like that so quickly. Zach figured it was his opportunity to witness to the doctor, so he shared the story of David in the Bible.

"You ever heard that story about David and Goliath, the giant? I believe I stepped into David's shoes today."

"What do you mean by that?" The doctor was unsure of the connection he was trying to make.

"For starters I am much smaller than Butch. And by all appearances Butch should have won that fight, but he walked off and had his thugs step in. His intent was to kill me and I'm still standing. David was a small young man, yet mighty in his faith and courage, which empowered him to defeat a giant with a single stone. Now, that seems impossible, yet he beat all the odds. My faith, as his, was placed entirely in God. It was God that strengthened me not to cower to the threat, I relied on Him to protect me and He had me outwit Butch. David struck out over a battlefield in the name of the Lord and killed the giant threat to his nation."

He was aware that he had the doctor's attention. "You know the Lord said to Samuel the prophet, in the Bible, '*Do not look at his appearance or at his physical stature, because I have refused him. For the LORD does not see as man sees; for man looks at the outward appearance, but the LORD looks at the heart* (1 Samuel 16:7 NKJV).' He saw a warrior and a king in the heart of David, yet a boy at the time, although Samuel had been looking at the stature of his brothers. God also sees something in my heart that was worthy of sending me here."

"You are here young man because you committed a crime that you are being held accountable for." The doctor thought he was stating the obvious.

"True, but that's not the whole story. I've already died, and I was sent back, not to serve a sentence, but to save lives from eternal agony."

"So, you are the one they have been talking about?" He had heard the stories being told, but now he met the young man being talked about and witnessed something amazing for himself.

"Apparently, I am. Do you know Jesus as your Savior?" Determined to talk about Jesus rather than himself.

It was clear that Zach was placed in the infirmary to witness to the doctor. They had a long conversation about Zach's testimony and about salvation. Zach could see how rewarding it was to witness to others. It was a comfort to know that he had reached at least two souls while in prison, the doctor and Joe.

The doctor was ready to release him back to his cell but encouraged him to come by any time, to let him check on his wounds. Although, Zach was aware that there was more that the doctor wanted to check on.

Joe had heard that he had been taken to the infirmary and assumed the worst. He knew something was up when they were separated. When Joe was able to lay eyes on Zach, he wanted to know what had happened, every detail. There was one question after another. Yet, the biggest one was how on earth was he sitting there with him after all that?

"It wasn't my day to die." Was the simple answer to all the questions.

"I guess you're going to tell me there is something in that Bible that explains today."

Smiling, he felt the Holy Spirit guide him to 2 Corinthians 4, as he read through it, he realized it was a message for him as much as it was a teaching for Joe. He began with 2 Corinthians 4 and carried over into Chapter 5 looking for a full message that would help them both understand the events of the day.

"'*We are hedged in (pressed) on every side [troubled and oppressed in every way], but not cramped or crushed; we suffer embarrassments and are perplexed and unable to find a way out, but not driven to despair; We are pursued (persecuted and hard driven), but not deserted [to stand alone]; we are struck down to the ground, but never struck out and destroyed; Always carrying about in the body the liability and exposure to the same putting to death that the Lord Jesus suffered, so that the [resurrection] life of Jesus also may be shown forth by and in our bodies.*

For we who live are constantly [experiencing] being handed over to death for Jesus' sake, that the [resurrection] life of Jesus also may be evidence through our flesh which is liable to death. Thus death is actively at work in us, but [it is in order that our] life [may be actively at work] in you (2 Corinthians 4:8-12 AMP).'"

Joe interrupted the reading to ask questions about what was being said. "So, are you going to be continually beaten to carry out your work here, Zach? Because I'm amazed that you survived what you went through today. I know who was throwing those punches and no one walks away from that. But you still had to have felt the blows and the pain. Why do you have to suffer like that?"

"Good question. I don't know the answer other than the fact that I know the Lord suffered much more for us. And He is still standing. Maybe it's to show that I will endure this and succeed in getting through to who the Lord is after. I know I shamed Butch, and this power struggle is not over. We are all going to die at some point in this journey of life, I just happen to know where I am going and what awaits me. Shall I continue?"

"Yes, please. Surely there is more for our understanding in there somewhere."

"'Yet we have the same spirit of faith as he had who wrote, I have believed, and therefore have I spoken. We too believe, and therefore we speak. Assured that He Who raised up the Lord Jesus will raise us up also with Jesus and bring us [along] with you into His presence. For all [these] things are [taking place] for your sake, so that the more grace (divine favor and spiritual blessing) extends to more and more people and multiplies through the many, the more thanksgiving may increase [and redound] to the glory of God (2 Corinthians 4:13-15 AMP).'"

"There's our answer. These things are actually taking place for my sake."

"Well, I have to say that's pretty strange. Here, let me torture you, it's for your own good?"

"No, I believe something good will come from all of it."

"Like what? More bandages being ordered?"

Zach chuckled at Joe's remark. "No. We will have to watch and see how things are revealed. But I'm pretty sure that's a Word for me. That good will come from all this." He continued to read, excited to see if more would be revealed.

"*'Therefore we do not become discouraged (utterly spiritless, exhausted, and wearied out through fear). Though our outer man is [progressively] decaying and wasting away, yet our inner self is being [progressively] renewed day after day* (2 Corinthians 4:16 AMP).'"

"Jesus actually told me something about that, when I was in heaven with Him. He talked about the renewing of my mind. I believe there are a lot of changes that occur when we trust in Him."

He picked up where he left off. "*'For our light, momentary affliction (this slight distress of the passing hour) is ever more and more abundantly preparing and producing and achieving for us an everlasting weight of glory [beyond all measure, excessively surpassing all comparisons and all calculations, a vast and transcendent glory and blessedness never to cease!], Since we consider and look not to the things that are seen but to things that are unseen; for the things that are visible are temporal (brief and fleeting), but the things that are invisible are deathless and everlasting* (2 Corinthians 4:17,18 AMP).'"

"So, we may not even be able to see what is going on?"

"Might not be meant for us to see, it's a spiritual thing happening. We will likely see the end result, on the other side."

Revelation was occurring as they read further. "*'For we know that if the tent which is our earthly home is destroyed (dissolved), we have from God a building, a house not made with hands, eternal in the heavens. Here indeed in this [present abode, body], we sigh and grown inwardly, because we yearn to be clothed over [we yearn to put on our celestial body like a garment, to be fitted out] with our heavenly dwelling, So that by putting it on we may not be found naked (without a body).*

For while we are still in this tent, we groan under the burden and sigh deeply (weighed down, depressed, oppressed)—not that we want to put off the body (the clothing of the spirit), but rather that we would be further clothed, so that what is mortal (our dying body) may be swallowed up by life [after the resurrection].

Now He Who has fashioned us [preparing and making us fit] for this very thing is God, Who also has given us the [Holy] Spirit as a guarantee [of the fulfillment of His promise]. So then, we are always full of good and hopeful and confident courage; we know that while we are at home in the body, we are abroad from the home with the Lord [that is promised us] (2 Corinthians 5:1-6 AMP).'"

Zach looked up from the book. "Jesus told me that things would not be easy. But He did promise that He would always be with me, and I believe I survived to fulfill my purpose, and because He promised I'd see this through with Him. It's also stated in John 16:33 (NASB), '*These things I have spoken to you, so that in Me you may have peace. In the world you have tribulation, but take courage; I have overcome the world.*' We can be overcomers too."

"Well, you certainly do have tribulation, we have one piece of the puzzle now, we know who the threat is coming from, that's a big part of the mystery, but when will they attack again. Now, we just have to make sure you are protected, so we can limit some of that suffering."

"God has already proven that He is good, He brought me someone like you to watch my back. Thanks Joe."

Song "That'll Preach" by Zach Williams

16
THE VISIT

The Chaplains and Pop had come to the conclusion that they had overstayed their visit with Miss Mae, although she kept making excuses for them to extend their stay. The list kept getting longer, of the things she needed help with, it was apparent she was good at stalling tactics. She had come to think that their stay was her new normal, she didn't want any of them to leave. The company was enjoyable and gave her an opportunity to serve others and be useful again. Miss Mae had always been an expert at manipulating people, the policeman and fireman had not made as many visits to her house since the Chaplains had been there. They had been the perfect solution to filling the long hours of the day.

Her loneliness had taken a backseat to caring for the family. The repair list was finished, Ellen had done the shopping and had Miss Mae stocked up with supplies, the list of chores had been accomplished. It was time to return home. Chris had his own jobs to tend to, and a need to replenish their finances had become imperative. Elsie would have packed Pearl, but she got caught. Ellen explained that Pearl needed to keep Miss Mae company. But Elsie insisted that Pearl was going to miss her, and she was just trying to keep her happy.

Although Pearl was not packed away, they were not leaving empty handed. Miss Mae had cooked up a feast to take with them, sandwiches for the road, a meal for when they made it home, and at least two pies and a cake were necessary to sustain them, so she expounded.

Miss Mae held back the tears that were to be shed later, lingering hugs were shared with each of them, as if it were the last time they'd see each other. They assured Miss Mae that they would be back to visit her again before she knew it. Elsie didn't make parting easy on any of them. She had become accustomed to all the extra attention she received from Miss Mae and the extended stay with Pop. They were all leaving with full hearts and gracious memories of Miss Mae's hospitality.

Miss Mae recited John 16:32 (NASB) to them to let them know she would be alright.

"Behold, an hour is coming, and has already come, for you to be scattered, each to his own home, and to leave Me alone; and yet I am not alone, because the Father is with Me."

That was a truer statement than Miss Mae realized. Pulling away from the house and heading back down the mountain stirred thoughts that Pop had not wanted to think about. He had enjoyed Miss Mae's company more than he realized. Now that he was headed home, he was faced with loneliness, himself. He also knew that a decision would have to be made about the cabin. Would they sell it, or rent it? Would they ever be able to overcome the events that took place there? Would those terrifying memories outweigh the happy ones, those that had been shared there for years?

The police had finished with their cabin as a crime scene, so they could return if they liked, but no one was quite ready for that. They were unsure of the feelings that would surface. It was decided that they didn't need to ride back up the mountain to the cabin, they wanted to leave the area with a good mindset.

There were more tears when they had to drop Pop off at his house. It was good to be together through the ordeal that they had been through. Now that they were separating, how were they going to process their emotions?

Getting settled back into their lifestyle and regular routine was harder than they thought. Chris kept thinking of other questions that he wished he had discussed with Zach. Now home, back to life prior to the cabin events, he felt unsettled and didn't know why. It was as if there was unfinished business back on the mountain. It wasn't something he could discuss with Ellen because he wasn't sure where to begin and how to communicate what he was feeling.

There were just more questions needing to be asked that he couldn't put his finger on. Chris was confident in what he believed; he knew he was a Christ follower. Did he not want to save a soul for the kingdom? Witnessing a miracle like Zach's resurrection was still being processed in his mind, how did that happen? Being told that his daughter was given a special gift to visit with Jesus, was still hard to comprehend. It was apparent that he was struggling with a spiritual reality. Not wanting to burden his family with his doubts, he felt that a visit to the prison would be in order, Zach may be able to help him understand some things. As soon as he got some things lined up and accomplished a few of his projects, he would schedule a trip.

Caught up in the moment of things, the cabin, the court case, staying at Miss Mae's, they just prodded through each day, but now that they were home, it allowed them too much time to think about all the events that had occurred, and it began to burden their hearts.

Ellen kept processing different scenarios in her head, how things could have gone differently, all the what ifs flooded her consciousness. She had too much time to think, which led to distress, making it difficult to sleep at night; nightmares were prevalent. Seeking Scripture for help, knowing that answers could be found within the pages of the Bible. But kept falling on ones that sounded more like how she was feeling versus how to deal with it.

Landing on Psalm 102:1-7 (NIV). *"Hear my prayer, LORD; let my cry for help come to you, Do not hide your face from me when I am in distress. Turn your ear to me; when I call, answer me quickly. For my days vanish like smoke; my bones burn like glowing embers. My heart is blighted and withered like grass; I forget to eat my food. In my distress I groan aloud and am reduced to skin and bones. I am like a desert owl, like an owl among the ruins. I lie awake; I have become like a bird alone on a roof."*

Feeling alone because she didn't want to burden Chris with her problems, he had enough on his plate trying to find enough work to bring their funds back up. What she was actually dealing with was not something she could discuss with anyone; it was an internal chaos. And she wasn't sure why.

Ellen's heart was more open to the five-fold ministry, embracing the miracle she witnessed was a gift from God, it confirmed her beliefs. Strengthened by the knowledge that Jesus was present and that He spoke to her child. What a blessing she felt from these experiences. She just needed something to calm her inner spirit, and focus on their survival, not reflect on the worse case scenarios that haunted her.

Elsie couldn't quit talking about Pearl and how much she was missing her. Ellen finally broke down and bought her a kitten to appease her, not realizing it may have been something she needed as well.

The new kitten was called Pearlene. When Ellen asked why, Pearlene? Elsie stated, because she had to be related to Pearl, couldn't her mom see the resemblance? There was no resemblance, other than they were both cats.

Pearlene turned out to be a comfort to them all, perhaps more to Ellen than she realized at first. Pearlene slept on top of Ellen at night, her purring was soothing to the soul, and she slept more comfortably. Her mind also went to Isaiah 41:10 (NIV) for comfort. "*So do not fear, for I am with you; do not be dismayed, for I am your God. I will strengthen you and help you; I will uphold you with my righteous right hand.*"

With time, and several good nights of sleep, she began to realize that Pearlene may have been the perfect gift she needed. Had Jesus played a part in that? She thanked Him one way or another. Time passed and they established a new normal for the family which included Pearlene.

Tea party Fridays resumed with Jesus. Ellen was rested and felt more like herself, now eager to assist in preparations for the Friday tea party. It was known now that Jesus really did have tea with her daughter, so more effort was put into what was served. The purchase of little tea crackers, more like cookies; finger sandwiches and actual tea was prepared versus water that she had Elsie serve before. Ellen sat in the next room, her heart overwhelmed by the thought that her daughter was having tea with Jesus, she listened carefully to what was discussed.

Hearing Elsie apologize, that it wasn't as fancy as the tea they had at Miss Mae's house, but Jesus didn't seem to mind. He enjoyed His visits with Elsie, her heart was always in the right place. Jesus was nurturing Elsie for greater purposes; teatime was a means to ensure a close relationship with her, so that she wouldn't lose her trust in her experiences with Him as she grows. Jesus shared with Elsie that her father was fixing to go on a trip, and he had a message for him to deliver to Zach. Elsie had not been used as a messenger except for the one time before, so she knew that it was important to remember what Jesus wanted to share with her.

Jesus was instructing her to encourage Zach to remember what had been said regarding his gifts. Jesus was confident that she would get the message delivered properly because he was aware that her mother was listening, but he spoke it to her slowly so that she would repeat it back to him.

"3:15, 3:15, is that right?" Elsie wanted to get it right, she remembered that she had reversed the numbers before.

Smiling at her effort and acknowledging she was doing a great job, while having her repeat the word, Mark. Jesus loves encouraging His children.

"Mark, Mark. I can remember the Mark. Like making a mark."

Jesus smiled and knew that she would remember in her own way, the message would be delivered. And of course, He knew Ellen was listening from the other room to confirm the key points. But it was important to encourage Elsie, so that she would feel more confident as she matured.

Ellen shared what she had overheard with Chris knowing that he would be seeing Zach at some point, but maybe it needed to be sooner than later. Chris pondered all that had been discussed and what had happened. He finally questioned Ellen as to why their child was selected to have tea with Jesus and promised to be used by Jesus in such a way?

"Why had He not used one of us? Look at how passionate you are about your faith, as well as being such a wonderful teacher, and have I not tried to evangelize wherever I am? It just doesn't seem to make sense to use a child."

Ellen responded with a smile, seeing the confusion in his face. "Our ways are not God's ways, and you actually answered yourself. You evangelize and I teach, those are our gifts, she has her own calling on her life. Does it not say in Romans 12, 'For as we have many members in one body, but all the members do not have the same function, so we, being many, are one body in Christ, and individually members of one another. Having then gifts differing according to the grace that is given to us, let us use them: if prophecy, let us prophesy in proportion to our faith; or ministry, let us use it in *our ministering; he who teaches, in teaching; he who exhorts, in exhortation; he who gives, with liberality; he who leads, with diligence; he who shows mercy, with cheerfulness* (Romans 12:4-8 NKJV).'"

"And is there one in there, one who always seems to have the right answers?" He smiled back at his wife, appreciating that she was helpful, not scolding him for not knowing that answer. Their daughter was destined to be a messenger of God.

The much-anticipated visit finally came around. Chris had gotten caught up enough with a few of his jobs, and had set aside time to visit Zach in prison. He made all the proper arrangements with the prison for a visit. It had been essential to keep in touch with Zach's lawyers, staying on him about the progress of having Zach moved to a less hardened prison. It was his hope to give Zach some good news. The report was not as positive as he would have liked.

Through a family update phone call, Ellen informed Pop of the trip being planned. This got Pop thinking that it was time for a road trip as he invited himself to go along for the ride. Explaining he would keep Chris company on the long drive, and it would give him an opportunity to visit with Miss Mae awhile. Figuring she would enjoy a little company.

The days had seemed longer without a companion around, someone to share a cup of coffee with. Although he had kept in touch with Miss Mae through several phone calls, they enjoyed their afternoon chitchats. However, this information had been kept to himself.

Chris wondered if there was more to this visit than meets the eye, was it to keep Miss Mae company or was it more like Pop was the lonely one? Genesis 2:18 (NIV), came to mind. *"The LORD God said, 'It is not good for the man to be alone. I will make a helper suitable for him."* He just smiled at Pop and said he would enjoy having him along for the ride.

Once again Miss Mae insisted that they stay with her. The road trip was too long to come and go in one day. She was thrilled to have company and meal plans were set in motion the moment she heard they were coming. It was settled, Pop could keep her company while Chris visited Zach, and they would spend the night, Miss Mae was once again managing the arrangements.

Headed back up the mountain wasn't as easy a trip as they thought it would be. Flashes of the events surfaced, neither one of them wanting to talk about it. They each processed it differently, yet both tried to be reminded of the positive things versus the emotional baggage that was heavy on their hearts. Pop, thinking that if it was going to be like this just headed up the hill, then he knew he wasn't wanting to reenter the cabin. He focused on his visit with Miss Mae, which brought a smile to his face.

The message had been delivered from Elsie to her father correctly. When Chris reflected on the verse, he became aware that Zach must be fighting demons in the prison. This would be something else he needed to question Zach about. Was his mission more than spreading the Gospel? Was he to rid the prison of some demons?

Zach lived his miracle; he had his own account to share. But the question was, how much had been revealed to him about heaven, about his gifts and abilities here on earth? How much time had he spent with Jesus? Chris remembered him saying that time was frozen, did he have any idea for how long? There were so many things he wanted to ask Zach, yet he also had information to deliver to him. Information that might help him survive prison. He hoped that the prison would allow him enough time to resolve some of his questions.

The reunion was well received, Zach was pleased to see Chris and elated to have a visitor, a friendly face. Chris wasn't sure where to begin but thought it best to deliver the message first, so as to not lose track of time and not be able to get it delivered. He wasn't sure if he would have a chance to return.

"Elsie was given a message from Jesus, to give to you. He said to read Mark 3:15 (NASB) and seek more understanding of the Word. It's a short verse, *'And to have authority to cast out the demons.'* Does that make sense to you?"

"Okay, I am fighting some pretty rough guys in here, but I hadn't considered them demons. Do you suppose they are possessed?"

"So, you've been in some fights?"

"Some little scuffles, but I've handled them for now." Zach was making light of what he had been through.

"They could be demon possessed. The Bible talks of such things. I don't think I really ever thought that was possible, but after what I have witnessed this year, I'm not sure what to believe. I think that's part of my visit, Zach. I was hoping you could fill me in more on what took place in heaven. I'm a Believer, but this new reality is kinda blowing my mind."

"I get it. I'm blown away by it when I think about it too much. I'm just walking in faith here. Taking one day at a time."

Zach continued to share some of what he remembered about heaven, but those memories were starting to fade a little.

"I think Jesus wants me to focus on the Word and to develop a stronger faith-walk with Him, versus relying on what I saw in heaven. Kind of like that verse in John 20:29 (NASB) *'Jesus said to him, 'Because you have seen Me, have you believed? Blessed are they who did not see, and yet believed.'*"

"You have already encouraged me, Zach. To think how different our lives were a few short months ago. I can't tell you how pleased I am that the Lord laid it on my heart to save your soul. I'm not so sure that it wasn't for both of us."

"Hey, I have you to thank for my life and my soul. I'm very grateful to all of you. Did I tell you; I think I've done the same for at least two souls here in this prison. My cellmate, and the doctor here." Zach was pleased to give a positive report on saving souls.

"That's great, Zach. It's quite the feeling to have witnessed to someone and know that you got through to them."

"Am I coming at it the right way, you think?" Zach felt that Chris could give him some pointers.

"You are doing just fine. You will not be able to reach them all, but if you reach one, it is worth the effort. You're proof of that. Just remember what is written about the one lost sheep."

Chris pulled out his Bible and opened it to Matthew 18:11-14 (NASB). *"'[For the Son of Man has come to save that which was lost.] What do you think? If any man has a hundred sheep, and one of them has gone astray, does he not leave the ninety-nine on the mountains and go and search for the one that is staying? If it turns out that he finds it, truly I say to you, he rejoices over it more than over the ninety-nine which have not gone astray. So it is not the will of your Father who is in heaven that one of these little ones perish.'* All humanity comes from God and are considered His children. He goes to extreme lengths to find any that are lost."

"Yes, that's why I'm here, to search for the lost that can be found."

"Speaking of here, I had hoped that I could bring you good news. It doesn't look like they are transferring you anytime soon." Chris hated to deliver a dark word versus something encouraging.

"I wouldn't want to be transferred. I believe I was placed here for a special purpose. These are the lost souls that God is searching for, I'm sure of it. He blessed me with friendship and security through my cellmate from the first day. What I am trying to say is that I'm where I'm supposed to be."

This was an unusual response from Zach but an encouraging one, that he felt this was where he was meant to be. Chris knew that the Lord was strengthening him.

"We are praying for your safety." Chris was concerned about hearing of his run-in and trip to the infirmary. Although Zach didn't share all the details.

"Let's get back to what the message was about. Do you have any insight into what I am supposed to do with that?" Zach wasn't sure what to do with the concept of demons.

"He did say seek the Word. I know there is another verse that says something similar, I believe Luke 9:1 (NASB) goes something like, '*And He called the twelve together, and gave them power and authority over all the demons and to heal diseases.*'"

Chris admitted, "I did some searching myself after Elsie gave me the message and what I think you need to be led to is John 14:26,27 (NASB), '*But the Helper, the Holy Spirit, whom the Father will send in My name, He will teach you all things, and bring to your remembrance all that I said to you. Peace I leave with you; My peace I give to you; not as the world gives do I give to you. Do not let your heart be troubled, nor let it be fearful.*'"

They both pondered the Word a minute. "I believe He wants to leave you with peace and understanding that the Helper is also with you, to teach you what He wants you to know. He will guide you to a deeper understanding. Maybe reflect more on what He said to you when you were with Him."

"Which brings to mind why did He send a message through Elsie? Why not just come to me and tell me in person?" Zach asked, a bit confused.

"Good question. One which I don't have a good answer for. Although I know that God puts a high value on the life of a child. They are a treasure to Him, because they have taken Him at His word, it's true faith that they demonstrate. Maybe He is seeking that from us." He paused then stated. "Yet, it may have been more for me than for you."

"What do you mean by that?"

"I've been struggling lately with a lot of this new spiritual realm, that we are all experiencing. I'm realizing that it's kind of outside my comfort zone. Maybe it was meant for me to be more involved in it, by having to deliver you a message, and realizing that Jesus is talking directly to my daughter. It's a lot for me to comprehend."

"I'll share a Psalm with you that may help you, then. I know that it gives me comfort and I recite it often, because I am thankful for what He has done for me."

Flipping to the Psalm in his Bible. "*Good and upright is the LORD; Therefore He teaches sinners in the way. The humble He guides in justice, And the humble He teaches His way. All the paths of the LORD are mercy and truth, To such as keep His covenant and His testimonies. For Your name's sake, O LORD, Pardon my iniquity, for it is great. Who is the man that fears the LORD? Him shall He teach in the way He chooses. He himself shall dwell in prosperity, And his descendants shall inherit the earth. The secret of the LORD is with those who fear Him. And He will show them His covenant.* (Psalm 25:8-14 NKJV).'"

Closing the book and looking up at Chris. "He is teaching me something new every day, and you are right, the Holy Spirit is guiding me to what I need to study and keep my focus on. I'm sharing my testimony with anyone that will listen, in hopes that they come to know the Lord, one sinner to the next. You already know the Lord, but He is trying to teach you something new, that you haven't allowed yourself to open-up to, His ways, not yours, Chris."

"That is a powerful message. There is a lot of truth in that. I do need to be more open minded." Things were starting to make a little more sense to him. Had he put limitations on God without realizing it?

Disappointment enveloped Zach when it was time to say goodbye. Chris promised to make another trip to update him on how things were going at home, and of course he wanted to be kept abreast of all that was happening inside the pen. Expressing how pleased Ellen would be that he was reaching those that needed Christ the most. Chris assured him he would send more Bibles to share with others and Ellen would send baked goods to sweeten the introductions to the Word. If all that was allowed, of course.

As Zach made his way back to his cell, Joe was there waiting for him. They loved getting news from the outside, so some information was shared about their visit to appease him.

Then Joe mentioned to Zach that he had been reading his Bible and came across something that he should hear, if he hadn't already read it. Feeling like it was a warning of some kind from this Book of his, as he put it. He opened it to 1 Peter 5:8-11 (AMP) and began reading.

"'Be well balanced (temperate, sober of mind), be vigilant and cautious at all times; for that enemy of yours, the devil, roams around like a lion roaring [in fierce hunger], seeking someone to seize upon and devour. Withstand him; be firm in faith [against his onset—rooted, established, strong, immovable, and determined], knowing that the same (identical) sufferings are appointed to your brotherhood (the whole body of Christians) throughout the world.

And after you have suffered a little while, the God of all grace [Who imparts all blessing and favor], Who has called you to His [own] eternal glory in Christ Jesus, will Himself complete and make you what you ought to be, establish and ground you securely, and strengthen, and settle you. To Him be the dominion (power, authority, rule) forever and ever. Amen (so be it).'"

"Sounds familiar, doesn't it?" Zach was thinking back to his attack from Butch. Which was the same thing that Joe had thought.

"Did you pick up on the fact that it says you are going to suffer a little while? Do you think that's done, or is there more to come?"

"I'm not sure, but I'll rest in the fact that He has dominion forever and I've been given a message that states that I also have authority given to me by Jesus. I've got some work to do, and I believe I will be encountering some pretty wicked stuff."

Zach flipped open the Bible. "I'm counting on that authority given to me here in Luke 10:19 (NASB), *'Behold, I have given you authority to tread on serpents and scorpions, and over all the power of the enemy, and nothing will injure you.'* Shall we be in agreement, that we have an enemy to take care of in here? I don't think it is as much man, as it is a demon spirit on men in here." An eerie feeling came over him.

"And you think you can cast them out of these men?" Joe asked with eyes wide open in a bit of fear.

"I'm planning on studying more about this and praying that the Holy Spirit will reveal more information to me. But I must believe it, for it to take place."

Song "Me On Your Mind" by Matthew West, Anne Wilson

17

THE POSSESSION

Zach continued to praise the Lord for all that He had given him and done for him. He praised Him for his salvation, a second chance to make things right, giving him the opportunity to serve Him, and to introduce others to Him. Praised Him for friendships like Chris, Ellen and now Joe. The more he had to praise the Lord about, the more he felt strengthened. He read through Psalm 9 often.

"I will praise You, O LORD, with my whole heart; I will tell of all Your marvelous works. I will be glad and rejoice in You; I will sing praise to Your name, O Most High. When my enemies turn back, They shall fall ad perish at Your presence. For You have maintained my right and my cause; You sat on the throne judging in righteousness. You have rebuked the nations. You have destroyed the wicked; You have blotted out their name forever and ever. The LORD also will be a refuge for the oppressed, A refuge in times of trouble. And those who know Your name will put their trust in You; For You, LORD, have not forsaken those who seek You (Psalm 9:1-5, 9,10 NKJV)."

When there is little else to do in a prison, it's the perfect time to focus on the Word and listen for guidance. Joe and Zach spent a lot of time in the Word, studying and seeking the answers they needed to carry on the ministry that the Lord asked of him. Zach was pleased to have a partner.

They read that when *"Two of you agree on earth concerning anything that they ask, it will be done for them by My Father in heaven* (Matthew 18:19 NKJV)." This was a comfort to them both. And it was believed that is why the Lord placed him in the cell with Joe.

As new believers and witnesses to the miraculous, Zach and Joe accepted what they studied in the Bible. Why would they doubt when Zach had been a part of the miracles himself. They had not been corrupted by what is considered Religion, which teaches limitations on the authority and power which Jesus left His disciples and was intended for every Believer.

It was clearly put in John 14:12-14 (NKJV), "*Most assuredly, I say to you, he who believes in Me, the works that I do he will do also; and greater works than these he will do, because I go to My Father. And whatever you ask in My name, that I will do, that the Father may be glorified in the Son. If you ask anything in My name, I will do it.*" This brought them comfort and assurance that they had been given abilities to do the Will of God.

Strength was needed for what he was about to encounter, and the support of Joe was much appreciated. Another ambush had been planned; the threat was spread throughout the prison to bring about fear, and anticipation. It was the day and time that was unknown.

Butch had revenge on his mind. He has been shamed before, when he had walked away from Zach, but this time he wasn't backing down and he wasn't taking Zach on by himself, they were going to gang up on him all at once. They were not planning on a need for the infirmary, just a body bag.

As much as Butch tried to keep the details of the ambush quiet, there were those that had heard Zach speak and didn't think that it was right what they had planned for him. They hadn't converted, but they knew that he was trying to help them, and some of his words had resonated with them. They got a warning sent down the pipeline to Joe, that the day had arrived, who got the message to Zach.

At this point, Zach was more concerned about Joe than for himself. If Joe stepped in to try to help him, he would get caught up in the bloodshed. It was unknown if his protections for his mission would also protect Joe who had partnered with him. Zach may have reached the one he was sent to evangelize to, now his own life may be jeopardized. It remained an unknown. There hadn't been any kind of confirmation on the ones the Lord was specifically trying to reach. Therefore, prayers went up to cover them both in safety.

"'*Incline Your ear to me, rescue me quickly; Be to me a rock of strength, A stronghold to save me. For you are my rock and my fortress; For Your name's sake You will lead me and guide me. You will pull me out of the net which they have secretly laid for me, For you are my strength. Into Your hand I commit my spirit; You have ransomed me, O LORD, God of truth* (Psalm 31:2-5 NASB).'"

The ambush took place in the dining hall. Doors were jammed with mop sticks and broom handles to prevent interruption from the guards. Joe and Zach were trapped, evil eyes were upon them.

The men Butch recruited were lined up in two rows creating a path for Butch to walk down the middle, to take his revenge out on Zach, and the rest would join suit after his first blow. As Butch started to make his way toward them, Zach jumped up on a table to be heard and to give the impression that he was not fearful. He was ready to take on the challenge.

He shouted with authority. "This location is much like the one mentioned in the Bible, *'And he cried out with a mighty voice, saying, 'Fallen, fallen is Babylon the Great! She has become a dwelling place of demons and a prison of every unclean spirit, and a prison of every unclean and hateful bird* (Revelation 18:2 NASB).' It's time for the bird to sing." Fearlessly staring down the threat in front of him.

"You've heard the miracles that have happened in my life, you've witnessed my recovery, yet you think you can destroy me. Do you think that I stand here alone? Think again."

They were thinking that Joe was his only backup, as they looked around the room. Figuring they had them outnumbered and out powered. They did not fear Joe standing with Zach. Yet the boldness in which he spoke unnerved them in the slightest way, which was an open door for Zach to push through.

"*'You believe that there is one God. Good! Even the demons believe that—and shudder.* (James 2:19 NIV).' You should shudder at what God can bring down on you."

Now there was an awareness that Zach was speaking of God's presence among them. These words had some of the bullies freeze up, even Butch slowed his pace. Fear could be smelled; it was so thick in the air some were choking on it. Some looked around the room to see if something was about to fall on them, the presence was so great.

Zach noticed this and half anticipated fire from heaven to fall, as well. Yet he needed to continue to capture their attention on his own and hopefully bring them to their knees. There were guards looking on, from closed doors through the glass windows, helpless to assist, or paid to stand back. Things were bustling in the halls outside the doors, word had gotten out that the event had started, and everyone was wanting to know how it was going.

More Scripture was spoken boldly to these men with what seemed like fire upon his words. Joe watched his back and stood there as if he knew exactly what Zach was going to do next, but he had no idea what was coming. He was determined not to show fear that would be like blood in the water.

"'*Submit therefore to God. Resist the devil and he will flee from you. Draw near to God and He will draw near to you. Cleanse your hands, you sinners; and purify your hearts, you double-minded* (James 4:7,8 NASB).' For truly I tell you, God is near! He has not forsaken me, and He wishes to draw you to Him. Do you wish to receive vengeance from the Lord or forgiveness?"

This kind of talk infuriated Butch. With fire in his eyes, he continued his march up between his men, who he thought had his back, until another miracle took place. Men, one by one, started to step in front of Butch to block his movement forward. He growled like a wild animal at them, which just made them all the more determined to block him.

Zach new that it was time to rebuke the demon that possessed Butch. The demon that had established Butch's power over the others. The one that had been ruling the prison from a cell, through threats and fear. Zach's eyes never left Butch as he shouted at the demon with great authority, claiming it had no power or authority to control any man, for it was to be trampled underfoot by man, who has been given authority by Jesus Christ, the Son of God.

The air in the room felt heavy, there was a certain evil present that made the hair on the back of one's neck stand up. Zach proceeded to cast the demon out and declare it vanquished to the darkness and dry place far from man. Declaring that it shall never return in Jesus' mighty name.

The men now backed away in fear of Butch, who was now writhing and twisting in an unnatural way, until he crumbled to the floor. He was cursing the Holy Spirit and shouting obscenities. He was flailing on the floor like a fish out of water, foaming at the mouth as if having a seizure while cursing Zach. He screamed, and then lay silent. Everyone was startled and feared what they had witnessed.

Zach spoke up with a strong voice showing no fear. "*But if it is by the Spirit of God that I drive out the demons, then the kingdom of God has come upon you [before you expected it]. Therefore I tell you, every sin and blasphemy (every evil, abusive, injurious speaking, or indignity against sacred things) can be forgiven men, but blasphemy against the [Holy] Spirit shall not and cannot be forgiven. And whoever speaks a word against the Son of Man will be forgiven, but whoever speaks against the Spirit, the Holy One, will not be forgiven, either in this world and age or in the world and age to come.*

You offspring of vipers! How can you speak good things when you are evil (wicked)? For out of the fullness (the overflow, the superabundance) of the heart the mouth speaks. The good man from his inner good treasure flings forth good things, and the evil man out of his inner evil storehouse flings forth evil things. But I tell you, on the day of judgment men will have to give account for every idle (inoperative, nonworking) word they speak. For by your words you will be justified and acquitted, and by your words you will be condemned and sentenced (Matthew 12:28,31,32,34-37 AMP).'"

Zach had studied these passages; he was prepared and thankful that Elsie had gotten him a message of warning from Jesus. He continued to speak to get through to the others.

"You have seen for yourselves what words can perform. But you need to know that Jesus spoke these words, '*I have not spoken on My own authority; but the Father who sent Me gave Me a command, what I should say and what I should speak* (John 12:49 NKJV)' and it is so with me, I have been told what to say, for it is written, '*When I speak with you, I will open your mouth, and you shall say to them, Thus says the Lord GOD. He who hears, let him hear; and he who refuses, let him refuse; for they are a rebellious house* (Ezekiel 3:27 NKJV).' This is surely a rebellious house and you have witnessed Butch's sentence. Will you not consider your next move more carefully? The kingdom of God is all around us, His power is present. Your admission to sin and your spoken word asking for forgiveness can acquit you from the same fate as this."

He pointed to Butch's lifeless body. "Act now while you have been given an opportunity."

The men fell to the ground scared of the presence and power of the Lord. Many lifting their hands up while on their knees asking to be forgiven. Outside the doors those that were witnessing what had taken place and what was being said also fell to their knees asking to be forgiven. Joe and Zach both were pleased and amazed at the same time.

The task was not done, Zach continued speaking to the men that were calling out for forgiveness from their knees.

"'*Giving joyful thanks to the Father, who has qualified you to share in the inheritance of his holy people in the kingdom of light. For he has rescued us from the dominion of darkness and brought us into the kingdom of the Son he loves, in whom we have redemption, the forgiveness of sins. The Son is the image of the invisible God, the firstborn over all creation. For in him all things were created: things in and on earth, visible and invisible, whether thrones or powers or rulers or authorities; all things have been created through him and for him. He is before all things, and in him all things hold together* (Colossians 1:12-17 NIV).'"

Looking at those on their knees, there was an eagerness to be forgiven.

"You have been delivered out of darkness; your response now is to call on the name of Jesus. Allow His peace to surround you. Many of you will never see the light of day outside these prison walls, but Jesus can free your mind from captivity through His peace. Declare that peace to your inner man and push back the external forces that have hardened your hearts."

Voices from all over the room were calling Jesus' name out loud. Grown men had been brought to tears. The doors opened and the guards came in to take control of the situation. They were amazed at how easily the men were subdued.

Whispers spread throughout the prison and many lives were changed, for the good. Inmates were asking to see Zach for counseling. His ministry was making a difference, creating a calmer, more peaceful environment behind prison walls. Word got back to the Warden how the facility was taking on a new life, all changes for the good. He approved a special room for Zach to carry on his ministry, trying to reach more men.

Chris heard of the success that Zach was having, and he made good on his promise to supply them with stacks of Bibles to the prison, which Zach handed out freely to those who were interested in studying on their own. There was deliverance of many kinds being conducted behind bars. These men were starting to seek something different for their lives, hope.

Song "Song of Deliverance" by Zach Williams

18

CLOSURE

God can use anyone that He sees fit to use for His purposes. It is demonstrated over and over in the Bible. He chose a lowly young man like Zach, a troubled youth, to reach men in the prison. He was one of them, could relate to their woes in life, yet he was redeemed and chosen to carry out a mission for God, to spread the Gospel behind bars. It taught Zach that God can look to the unspectacular to take center stage for something spectacular. His ministry made a difference in the lives of those who were held in prison for life, and for those who were to reenter society. Words were spoken to them about listening intently to the Holy Spirit. Obey what aligns with God's character and His Word, and they will live a more peaceful, productive, complete life, free from darkness. They too can be used by God as well.

Zach was so successful with his ministry that the Warden wanted to transfer him to another prison to have the same effect on the inmates there. He hated leaving his partner, Joe, who had been such a blessing to him and a big help in the ministry. Yet, Joe was expected to continue the work they started at this facility, while Zach started all over again in new surroundings.

It was almost automatic how the men came seeking counsel from Zach, searching for guidance when they heard his testimony and the success he had at the other prison. Many of these men had never heard the Gospel, no one bothered to share with them. Zach was telling them that

God loved them and that they could live differently with a better attitude, even in captivity.

As a reward for the good work Zach had been doing, he had been offered to be transferred to a more moderate prison, to fulfill his sentence. Trying to negotiate with the Warden, Zach insisted that his work would be better served in a more hardened prison, where all hope was felt lost. But the Warden insisted he be transferred. Zach really didn't have a say in the matter. But he decided that it must be a gift from the Lord because the Warden was so emphatic about it.

Wherever Zach landed he remained in touch with Chris on a regular basis. Zach appreciated Chris's contact, he found that he needed an element of insight from the outside world, realizing one day he would be free from the prison walls, he wanted it to be a smooth transition so that he could share with others how it was achieved.

Through their limited conversations he wanted to know all about their lives as well, how Elsie was doing, asking had she continued talking with Jesus. There were discussions as to what type of work Zach would do outside of the prison. Chris had hopes of taking Zach on as an apprentice, to assist him with his business, when he was released from prison. That was yet to be determined. Zach's priority would always be his ministry.

When he finished his sentence, Chris and Ellen had promised to help him get settled in the community near them. They recognized it as an opportunity to assist him further in his ministry, outside the prison walls. With their contacts and their combined testimony, they could open doors for him. It was felt that he would continue his ministry, just in a new way.

It was simply a new opportunity to reach out to those who have recently been released from prison. Knowing that these men would have a hard time adjusting outside the pen, and they would need assistance in many ways, they were needing new paths to follow, but spirituality was the most important topic to be covered with them.

God would have Zach doing a new thing just as it was said in Isaiah 43:19 (NASB), "Behold, I will do something new, Now it will spring forth; Will you not be aware of it? I will even make a roadway in the wilderness, Rivers in the desert."

Chris continued to encourage him to listen to God for guiding his next moves, he felt like God was preparing to do something unique with his ministry. Not that Zach needed to be reminded to look to the Word, but Chris directed him to verses where God mentioned fresh starts. Assuring him that God was pouring out new blessings on him just as it is stated that God can't pour new wine into old wine skins. He had to move forward.

"Therefore if anyone is in Christ, he is a new creature; the old things passed away; behold, new things have come (2 Corinthians 5:17 NASB)."

Prompting him with the fact that the men he would be working with will need to hear, "'*Then I will give them one heart, and I will put a new spirit within them, and take the stony heart out of their flesh, and give them a heart of flesh, that they may walk in My statutes and keep My judgements and do them; and they shall be My people, and I will be their God* (Ezekiel 11:19,20 NKJV).'"

There were other changes taking place as well. George made the decision to rent the cabin for income, rather than sell it. Renters didn't need to know the events that had taken place there, but to put it on the market, all would have to be disclosed and would make it difficult to sell. The income would be good for him now and a nice inheritance for Ellen and her family later.

As time passed, maybe they would be able to enjoy the cabin again. As tragic as the story at The Cabins had been, people were drawn to the mountain, out of curiosity. Renting the cabin had not been difficult even if they had heard the story of events on the mountaintop.

After multiple trips to the mountain to make the proper arrangements to rent his cabin, George was able to stay with Miss Mae and found pleasure in their companionship. Although a little older than himself, she gave him a run for his money. They enjoyed doing the chores around the house together, spending time over a cup of coffee, and catering to Pearl, the cat. A new mountain destination for the family was established at Miss Mae's where they all created wonderful memories.

A little over a year passed by when George proposed to Miss Mae. He decided it was time to make it more of a permanent situation, than extended visits. Chris and Ellen were not too surprised by the turn of events. It was apparent that he had been lonely and so had Miss Mae, with them enjoying each other's company so much, it was the natural progression of things. Everyone was happy to welcome her into the family officially.

There were other important decisions that had to be made in the family. Chris had thoughts of joining the ministry but felt that he could minister more to people out in the field than behind a pulpit. He believed that Jesus meant for the Gospel to be spread by example and that took rubbing shoulders with people where they are in life. Chris's business flourished which kept him quite busy and he was able to make many contacts for Jesus. A day didn't go by that he wasn't sharing the Gospel with someone.

Ellen remained busy homeschooling Elsie and conducting her own home Bible Study for women. The connection built up between the women carried over to assisting others in the community. Many were drawn to their family's story, but it had not been shared about Elsie's gift out of protection for her at this stage in her life.

Elsie continued her tea parties with Jesus on Fridays, and Jesus continued to share stories to teach Elsie about Himself and about God the Father. She found that if her mother had questions about Scripture meanings, she could ask Jesus directly for more insight into the Word. He always answered her in a way in which she could understand and remember. And she loved sharing with her mother what she had learned. Jesus was training her, but more importantly he was continually building their relationship.

Trips to heaven would commence soon, and it was His intent that she be able to remember what she saw to share with others. *"Train up a child in the way he should go, And when he is old he will not depart from it* (Proverbs 22:6 NKJV)."

The first thing that Zach wanted to do when he was released was to visit his mother in prison. There had been a strong conviction case against her, which carried a life sentence. There was no indication of remorse for anything she had done, so the walls seemed to close in on her existence. It was Zach's wish to demonstrate God's love towards her and his hope to witness to her, after all she was his mother.

Out of an expression of love, Zach wanted her to know that he forgave her for the abusive upbringing, and for dragging him into a life of crime. It was all she knew, and he realized she had done the best she could.

Louise had tried to escape her own abusive lifestyle but had gone at it the wrong way. Her choices led to the loss of one child, but her second child was alive and wanting her to know Jesus, the one who died for all, so that she wouldn't have to suffer torment. Trying to share that there is freedom from her sins, through the One that stands with open arms if she would only accept Him. Jesus could show her life free from her own captivity and enslaved mindset.

Sharing his own testimony with her hoping that it would enlighten her. Having heard the stories that ran through the prison, she was still pleased to hear it directly from Zach, it was a bit more meaningful. He told her of the work he had accomplished behind bars, about the many men that came to know Jesus and the difference it had made in their lives. He wanted her to be forgiven.

A well-used Bible was slid in front of her while his hand was still laying on the Bible, stating that he had marked passages that would help lead her to her own salvation. He offered his help when she was ready to accept it. Asking if she would like him to make regular visits to see her?

Without replying, she smiled at her son, laid her own hand on top of his and squeezed it for only a moment. Then gathered the Bible up to her chest as if she was clinging to it. She rose up and walked away without a word.

Song "Forgiven" by Crowder

ENDNOTES

Scripture quotation marked (NKJV) are taken from the NEW KING JAMES VERSION, Copyright ©1982 by Thomas Nelson, Inc.

Scripture quotation marked (NASB) are taken from the NEW AMERICAN STANDARD BIBLE, Copyright ©1960, 1971,1977, 1995, 2020 by the Lockman Foundation.

Scripture quotation marked (NIV) are taken from THE HOLY BIBIE, NEW INTERNATIONAL VERSION, Copyright ©1973, 1978, 1984, 2011 by Biblica, Inc.

Scripture quotation marked (AMP) are taken from the AMPIFIED BIBLE, Copyright ©1958, 1964, 1965, 1987 by the Lockman Foundation and Zondervan.

Scripture quotation marked (ESV) are taken from THE HOLY BIBLE, ENGLISH STANDARD VERSION, Copyright ©2001 by Crossway, a publishing ministry of Good News Publisher.

Scripture quotation marked (NLT) are taken from THE HOLY BIBLE, NEW LIVING TRANSLATION, Copyright ©1996, 2004, 2007 by Tyndale House Foundation.

Esther 9:1   NKJV
Revelation 11:12   NKJV
Hebrews 11:16   NASB
John 14:2   NIV
1 Peter 1:4,5   NKJV
Song "Soul Worth Saving" by Apollo LTD

Chapter 3
Psalm 25:16-20   NASB
Psalm 91:1-16   NIV
John 8:12   NASB
Poem "A Beacon Of Light" by Phil Soar, poemhunter.com

1 Timothy 5:5   NASB
Psalm 38:8-10   NIV
Song "Brighter Days" By Blessing Offor

Chapter 4
Ephesians 6:1-3   NIV
Song "Come As You Are" by Crowder

Chapter 5
Luke 1:37   NKJV
Isaiah 43:2,3   NKJV
2 Corinthians 6:17   NASB
Proverbs 13:20   NIV
2 Corinthians 3:4-6   NASB
Ephesians 6:10-12   NASB
Daniel 3:17   AMP
Song "Hear Of God" by Zach Williams

Chapter 6
Song "God Really Loves Us" by Crowder

Chapter 7

Philippians 2:9-11	NIV
John 3:16	NIV
John 11:25,26	NASB
Romans 6:23	NASB
Ecclesiastes 12:5-7	NKJV
John 14:2,3	NKJV
Isaiah 30:18	NASB
Psalm 9:7-10	NASB
Deuteronomy 32:4	NKJV
2 Corinthians 12:9	NKJV
Psalm 40:29-31	NASB
Romans 12:2	NIV84
Exodus 4:12	NKJV
Jeremiah 1:7,8	NKJV
Isaiah 55: 6-11	NIV84
Joshua 1:8,9	NKJV
Matthew 16:19	NKJV
Luke 21:13-15	NKJV
John 10:9,10	NKJV
Psalm 28:7-9	AMP
John 16:33	NKJV
Isaiah 41:10-13	NASB
Proverbs 2:1-5	NIV84
Psalm 105:4,5	NKJV

Song "Love Me Like I Am" by For King & Country, Jordin Sparks

Chapter 8

Psalm 19:14	NASB
Psalm 20:1,2	NASB
1 Corinthians 6:14	NASB
Luke 9:1,2	NASB

Matthew 10:7,8	NASB
Acts 4:30	NASB
1 Peter 2:23-25	NASB
Luke 7:13-15	NKJV
Philippians 4:13	NASB
Isaiah 12:2	NASB
Ephesians 6:10	AMP

Song "In Jesus Name (God of Possible)" by Katy Nichole

Chapter 9

Genesis 48:11	NASB
Psalm 133:1	NKJV
Psalm 145:4-7, 18-21	NKJV
Acts 16:31	NKJV
Deuteronomy 26:11	NKJV
1 Corinthians 7:14	NLT

Song "Who You Say I Am" by Hillsong Worship

Chapter 10

Deuteronomy 18:18,19	NASB
Jeremiah 17:7	NIV
Acts 4:29,30	NIV
Isaiah 60:1,2	NKJV
Ephesians 1:11-23	NASB
Romans 8:14-17	NIV
Exodus 20:16	NKJV
Proverbs 19:9	NKJV
Psalm 35:4-24	NIV

Song "Eye Of The Storm" by Ryan Stevenson

Chapter 11

Exodus 23:1	NASB
Zechariah 8:17	NASB

Proverbs 19:5   NKJV
Proverbs 25:18   NASB
Matthew 19:18   NKJV
2 Chronicles 20:7   NIV
Psalm 24:7-19   NIV
Song 'Better Days Coming' by MercyMe

Chapter 12
Psalm 143:20   NIV
Psalm 33:13,14   NIV
John 15:7   NIV
Romans 10:13-15   NIV
Song "You Are God Alone" by Rikki Doolan

Chapter 13
Psalm 50:1-14   NIV
2 Thessalonians 3:3   NASB
Exodus 7:3   NASB
Malachi 3:6   NKJV
Song "New Creation" by Mac Powell

Chapter 14
Philippians 4:6-9   NIV
Luke 10:19,20   NASB
Romans 12:12   NIV
Romans 12:14-19,21   NASB
Psalm 40:1-5   NASB
Luke 4:18   NIV
Psalm 102:27,28   NIV
Psalm 32:1-11   NIV
Proverbs 28:13   NASB
Jeremiah 33:2,3,6,8,9 NIV

Song "Nobody" by Casting Crown, ft Matthew West

Chapter 15

Romans 8:35-39	NIV
1 Samuel 16:7	NKJV
2 Corinthians 4 :8-12	AMP
2 Corinthians 4 :13-15	AMP
2 Corinthians 4 :16	AMP
2 Corinthians 4 :17,18	AMP
2 Corinthians 5:1-6	AMP
John 16:33	NASB

Song "That'll Preach" by Zach Williams

Chapter 16

John 16:32	NASB
Psalm 102:1-7	NIV
Isaiah 41:10	NIV
Romans 12:4-8	NKJV
Genesis 2:18	NIV
Mark 3:15	NASB
John 20:29	NASB
Matthew 18:11-14	NASB
John 14:26,27	NASB
Psalm 25:8-14	NKJV
1 Peter 5:8-11	AMP
Luke 10:19	NASB

Song "Me On Your Mind" by Matthew West, Anne Wilson

Chapter 17

Psalm 9:1-5,9,10	NKJV
Matthew 18:19	NKJV
John 14:12-14	NKJV
Psalm 31:2-5	NASB

Revelation 18:2   NASB
James 2:19   NIV
James 4:7,8   NASB
Matthew 12:28,31,32,34-37 AMP
John 12:49   NKJV
Ezekiel 3:27   NKJV
Colossians 1:12-17   NIV
Song "Song of Deliverance" by Zach Williams

Chapter 18
Isaiah 43:19   NASB
2 Corinthians 5:17   NASB
Ezekiel 11:19,20   NKJV
Proverbs 22:6   NKJV
Song "Forgiven" by Crowder

ABOUT THE AUTHOR

Partnered with the Holy Spirit, on an assignment from God to get different messaging points out through works of fiction. Jayda Lee Wilson has discovered her purpose for this season of her life. Preparation came through many years of Women's Bible Study, twenty years of teaching children the basic principles of the Bible, to facilitating a small women's group in studies, as well as leading devotions for a Women's Circle. Moving on to a new focus of listening intently to the Holy Spirit's guidance, being led to write down what is revealed in dreams from the Lord and developing them into works of fiction. Known to be creative from her career days as an interior designer, writing was never in her sights until she was inspired to write devotions, which honed her skill in listening and being guided by the Lord through the process of now creating published works which include "The Jump", "Return To The City", "Life Choices -Assignment From God", "The Little Messenger" and authored many more. Having traveled many of the United States and various spots around the world with family and friends, her favorite destination is home with her beloved pets and time spent with her grandchildren.

Printed in the United States
by Baker & Taylor Publisher Services